Mystery Box

Mystery Box

Gordon McAlpine

Cricket Books
A Marcato Book
Chicago

Text copyright © 2003 by Gordon McAlpine
All rights reserved
Printed in the United States of America
First American Edition, 2003
Designed by Anthony Jacobson

The Library of Congress Cataloging-in-Publication data for *Mystery Box* is available under LC Control Number 2003002036

To Jonathan, Shane, and Harlan,
who have taught me much about
kindness and courage

Contents

Introductory Note

Between 1927 and 1930, publisher Edward Strate-
meyer introduced to the reading public the first of
the Hardy Boys and Nancy Drew mystery novels.
Since then, the two series have entertained millions of young readers. The authors of these books,
Franklin W. Dixon and Carolyn Keene, never lived
in a real-world, tax-paying sense; rather, the names
Dixon and Keene are pseudonyms for the many
ghostwriters who for generations have spun sus-
penseful tales of two brothers from Bayport and a
bold girl from River Heights.

But who might Franklin W. Dixon and Carolyn
Keene have been if they had been real?

A mystery . . .

What follows is the solution.

PART ONE

The truth is, not every member of the "lost generation" was actually lost. No, some among those who lived and worked in Paris during the 1920s eventually found themselves by finding their life's work—or by finding one another. Or both. For example, I recall Franklin Dixon and Carolyn Keene. They eventually wrote those popular mystery series for boys and girls. Novels of hardy boys and a titian-haired girl detective. Not the most refined literature, perhaps. But their lives . . . well, Frank and Carolyn's lives were their best stories.

—Gertrude Stein in conversation

Bayport, 1918

All was as silent as the tomb save for the distant
pounding of the sea upon the cliff.

Franklin W. Dixon
The House on the Cliff

A motorcycle roared up the Old Mill Road, which began at
the edge of Bayport, Connecticut. The road passed through
the scrub brush outside town and continued past the Morton
farm and up into the woods. There, the road traversed a
steep incline. Two motorcyclists had once raced along this
twisting part of the road. They had sometimes caught
glimpses through the trees of one another seeming to travel
in opposite directions, though they would shortly arrive at
the same place. Now, only one bike ascended, its motor
steady in the stillness. At the far edge of the woods, the road
turned once more back toward town, like a snake pursuing
its own tail. The final incline was long and straight, ending
on a rocky promontory that overlooked Bayport and the
glimmering Atlantic. In all, it was not more than a mile from
the edge of the promontory to Bayport's City Hall, which

1

from this height looked little larger than the model buildings of a toy train set—a mere mile as the crow flies. However, it was almost twenty miles by motorcycle. For Frank Dixon, these miles had never seemed longer; he'd have believed that the time spent on this journey was easily equal to the nineteen years that to then had comprised his life. Nonetheless, when he skidded to a dusty stop near the edge of the cliff, he knew he was not ready for what lay ahead. No matter. Frank Dixon had learned that what lay ahead had no regard for one's preparedness.

He switched off the Indian V-twin and swung one leg over the leather seat of the bike, which like his brother's had been a Christmas gift three years before. He set the stand. His face was windblown from the ride, red but for the white around his eyes and brows where his goggles, which hung now around his neck, had pressed into his skin. His hair was swept at odd angles about his head. He took a long breath. Frank Dixon was known all over Bayport for his boundless energy. His brother too. The Dixon boys.

That was all past.

Bayport lay below. Frank recognized each of its shingled buildings; it was the town where he and his family had lived all these years. From here, Bayport was serene, more an idea than a place. Americans would leave their homes by the thousands to move to this town if they saw it from this angle, Frank thought. Postcard perfect with white boats bobbing in the harbor. However, all of America would be coming to Bayport without knowing the first thing about it; they would be coming not for the actual town but for its picturesque representation. Frank Dixon had come to know that the image of a thing was never the thing itself. Nor was its name. Otherwise, Frank would not feel so alone. He could merely take the photograph of Joe out of his wallet and look at it. He could merely speak his brother's name. But Frank had already tried these things and had learned that neither a picture nor a word could be his brother. Nothing was his brother. Frank unstrapped the black saddlebag over the bike's rear fender. He removed a wooden box little bigger than an ostrich egg. Then he turned to the sea far below.

Alone now.

In the past, Frank and Joe had come here together. Their friends too. Here they had smoked cigarettes and sometimes passed a bottle of Canadian whiskey with such reverence that the act took on the air of communion, at least until one of them vomited. The last time Frank and Joe were here together was nine months before; Joe had dropped out of high school to enlist. After training in the U.S. Army's School of Aeronautics in Ohio, he would be off to the front lines in France, where the Dixon brothers—like all their friends—believed a bold boy could become a bold man. On Joe's last day here in Bayport, he had been less concerned with enemy pilots and antiaircraft fire than with the diplomats who might find a way to end the war before he had a chance to get to it.

"To be so close to a real adventure, and then have it all end," Joe worried, gazing over the Atlantic, as if from three thousand miles away he might see streaks of artillery fire or the black smoke of explosions from the muddy fields of France.

"We've had real adventures," Frank suggested. "You and me."

Joe nodded. He and Frank were known about Bayport as amateur detectives. Their father, Fenton, was a retired N.Y.P.D. inspector who worked now as a private investigator for the Mutual Insurance Corporation. His stories of crime had years before fueled the boys' imaginations. Together, they had helped a local man recover a hidden will, returning a large estate to its rightful heir, and later had helped expose a smuggling ring that was using the old mill as its hideout. From the bushes, they had watched local authorities raid the place, killing in a bloody barrage all those hidden inside.

Joe motioned across the sea. "Imagine being with Alexander's army. Or Napoleon's. That's what's happening over there now."

"Since when did you become a war buff?" Frank asked.

Joe smiled, his eyes sparkling in the sun. "It's just Mr. White's history class."

"You mean the class you got a C-minus in?"

Joe laughed. "So I'm not great at remembering names and dates. Big deal. If I'd stuck around for the whole semester, I'd have gotten the grade up. Besides, there's never been a date in history more important than today. Provided I get through flight training in time to get there."

"I don't want to hear about it," Frank answered. He too would have enlisted, but the army would not have him. As a child, he had broken his right leg; set improperly, it had failed to keep pace with the growth of the left leg, leaving him now with one orthopedic shoe that compensated for the difference with an additional inch and a half of rubber sole. Growing up, he had never allowed the difference to stop him from playing games with the other boys. He could always run, just not very fast. He could always jump, just not very high. Walking, he barely betrayed a limp. But the United States Army was no place for exceptions.

"Oh, you're doing great things too," Joe said.

Frank brushed his brother's compliment away with a wave of his hand.

"I mean it," Joe continued, "The first Dixon to attend college. You think that's no great shakes? Come on, Frank, you know how proud Mom and Dad are. Come September when you start at Princeton you're going to be a hero around here. And I'm proud of you too."

"Yeah, yeah," Frank muttered.

The boys cast stones off the promontory toward the sea.

"Don't get me wrong," Joe continued. "I wish you were coming. We'd be unstoppable together. You know that. Von Richthofen and his flying circus would turn tail at the sight of us!"

"Yeah, we've been quite a team, Joe."

"The Dixon boys."

"We still are quite a team."

"Damn right."

"Joe, it's not too late for you to change your mind."

"About what?"

"You could stay here and finish high school," Frank said.

"No."

"You could get your diploma," Frank continued. "It's only one more year."

"You're the student, Frank. Not me. You're the future lawyer. Everybody says so."

"I don't want to be a lawyer."

"That's not the point."

Frank said nothing.

"Tell me, Frank, what would you do if you were me?"

Frank looked away.

"Well?" Joe pressed.

Frank did not answer but tossed a rock at his younger brother.

"Punk," Joe said, laughing as he dodged the rock.

At first, Joe wrote to Frank from Ohio every day. Soon, however, the pressures of flight school became overwhelming and his letters became less detailed, then less frequent, then nonexistent. Frank understood. Each week, elimination exams sent disappointed waves of flight-school recruits into the infantry. Frank had heard enough about the infantry to know that there was nothing adventurous about dying of dysentery in the trenches. Joe knew too, which is why he awoke each day at 3:45 a.m. to study in the latrine, the only place at that hour with enough light to read by. A grade of C-minus might have been sufficient in Mr. White's history class, but not in flight school. In the cockpit, things came easier for Joe. He was a natural flier. After nine weeks he passed his exams and was commissioned as a second lieutenant, assigned to the 27th Aero Squadron. At last, he wrote to his brother:

> . . . The best of all, Frank, is to feel when I'm flying that the muscles of my arms and legs actually extend to the wings and tail of the machine, so that all I have to do is think about where I want to go and the airplane will follow, the way your hand balls up without effort just by your thinking "fist." Sure, I move the stick with my hand and the rudder bar with my feet, but I become no longer aware of doing so. Only the machine knows. And I just fly.

In France, Joe's exuberance intensified, at first.

> . . . We wheel around each other in tight turns, watching all the time, circling like boxers, waiting for the other to drop his guard, waiting for a clean shot. A knockout punch. Then the Hun pilot makes a stall turn and a dive, and you follow, and the rolling and zooming starts over again. Round two.

You pepper little jabs just to let the bastard know you're there. Little bursts of machine-gun fire. Meantime, you're waiting for the real opening, waiting for the knockout punch. You have to be patient but relentless. Of course, this is no boxing ring. No, this championship bout takes place in the air, in three dimensions. Left, right, forward, back, up, down. All the time looking for your opening. Then, the Hun makes a mistake. Your opening! And then it's hard on the machine gun. Rat-a-tat-tat!

Oh Frank, when I actually see one of those Hun airplanes it's gonna be so sweet!

His last letters to Frank (which differed from the more optimistic letters he continued to write to their mother and father) included grim stories of infantry used as fodder to gain mere yards in one or another offensive. Joe himself did not experience life in the trenches. Rather, he lived behind the lines with other pilots in relative comfort. At night they sang and drank wine. Joe even became involved in a romance, though details remained in shadow. By day, however, Joe was assigned the task of shooting down German observation balloons, which were usually fortified by heavy ground cover and enemy aircraft. It was not long before he had accomplished his first official kill. Then another. And another.

When your moment finally comes and a Fokker is diving out of the sun straight for you, your training and concentration drive away the fear. If not, you're done for. There's no time to think. All your tension and concentration come together with a leap of your heart.

Your body tightens in the straps, and your thumb goes to the gun button. You make an evasive maneuver, applying a little flap to pull a tighter circle, and then you get on the Hun's tail. By this time, your heart is ice. All calculated. Truth is, Frank, it's not as thrilling as you'd imagine. It doesn't feel like fistfighting. There's no blood lust, just technique. At least, that is, until after you've shot the poor bastard out of the sky. Then something happens like exaltation, savage and intense. It sweeps over you. It's not a feeling to be proud of, but I guess you can't avoid it.

Then Joe wrote no more.

A one-armed army captain visited the Dixon family. He told them that Joe's barracks had been hit in the dead of night by a seventy-millimeter shell fired from ten miles away out of the barrel of a massive German weapon known as "Big Bertha." Seconds later, another shell hit the airfield's fuel dump and the already damaged barracks became engulfed by flames. None of the men sleeping inside survived. The captain described the sequence of events as "bloody bad wartime luck."

To Frank, it was the end of his world.

Extended family gathered in the Dixon house. Friends too. Chet Morton, Tony Prito, Phil Cohen, and many others from Bayport High School. And townsfolk, some of whom had known Joe his whole life. The Women's Auxiliary brought platters of food. All spoke in respectful tones; nonetheless, a bittersweet lightness sometimes emerged when one or another of the guests recalled Joe's imagination or courage. Something of his best attributes remained in Bayport, like the scent of a flower whisked into another room. Men spoke of patriotism and sacrifice, but none of the women seemed much interested in those words. Frank wasn't interested in them either. That Joe had taken this-or-that number of Germans with him made little difference to Frank. Better were the stories of Joe as a child, which his aunts and uncles related.

Laura Dixon remained secluded in her room.

Fenton Dixon straightened his posture and acted the host.

A few days later, when all the visitors had gone, the army captain visited again. His manner was changed. He had new information. Joe's remains had not been identified among the victims of the attack, he informed them.

"What does that mean?" Laura Dixon asked, rubbing at her red, swollen eyes, as if seeing more clearly might help her to understand.

"Are you saying he's not dead?" Fenton Dixon asked.

"That's right."

"Then where is he?" Laura asked.

"Your son must have deserted his post under fire," the captain answered. "We don't know where he is now."

"But he's alive?" Laura cried.

"For now," the captain said.

"What does that mean?" Frank asked.

"We're looking for him," the captain explained. "Desertion is a capital offense."

"What? No!" Laura cried.

"Joe would never desert," Frank said. "You've made a mistake."

"I'm afraid not, young man."

"Your visit here last week was a mistake," Fenton said. "Perhaps you've made another."

"The bodies were badly burnt, which made identification unusually complicated."

"Maybe Joe was sent on a secret mission," Frank suggested.

The captain shook his head.

"The boy was no coward," Fenton Dixon said.

"War ennobles some," the captain answered. "We've all heard stories of cowardly youngsters who find hidden reserves of courage under fire. Well, sometimes it works the other way around."

"What are you suggesting?" Frank asked.

"Until we find your brother, our official position is that Lieutenant Dixon perished with his comrades," the captain said. "This is a delicate time, politically. An armistice may be near. The War Department is aware of your distinguished service record in the Spanish-American War, Mr. Dixon. Your son's future is uncertain. However, the Western Front is no place for a fugitive to be slinking about. Land mines, artillery, stray bullets. I didn't come here to give you false hope. He may already have been rounded up in a sweep of deserters and shot on the spot."

"No!" Laura said.

"It would not be a miscarriage of justice," the captain replied.

"Get out," Fenton Dixon said.

"I was under no order to come here." The captain placed his hat on his balding head as he rose to leave. "I just thought you folks should know the truth about your son."

"Thank you," Fenton replied.

"The truth, for better or worse," the captain concluded.

"What are we going to do?" Laura asked after the captain left the house.

"There's nothing to be done," Fenton answered.

"There has to be something," Frank said.

"No. We do nothing at all."

"I must call Aunt Gertrude," Laura said, turning away and starting for the telephone.

"Stop!" Fenton called, his hands running nervously through his thick, gray hair.

"What is it?"

"I told you. You're to do nothing."

"I don't understand," she said.

"Sit down, both of you," Fenton Dixon ordered.

Frank sat beside his mother.

"This is all happening so fast," Fenton said. "We have to take a moment to absorb this new information. Then we have to ask ourselves what's best."

"What's best is that Joe's alive," Frank answered. Nothing could be simpler, he thought.

"Maybe he's alive," Fenton said. "Maybe he isn't."

"But this news gives us hope," Frank replied.

"And it would give others in this town ammunition to use against us."

"What are you saying, Dad?"

"I'm saying that since we have no definite word of Joe's whereabouts or condition, we should carry on as if today's visit never happened."

"But it did happen," Laura said.

"Yes, but to what end?" Fenton asked. "After all, Joe is still dead to us."

"How can you say that?" Laura demanded.

"One is dead when one's heart stops working," he replied. "And when one's courage deserts, one's heart has stopped working. It's simple logic. You're the one going to college, Frank. You work it out for your mother."

"Are you calling Joe a coward?" Frank asked.

"I think it's best for everybody in this town to continue assuming he died honorably."

"I don't care what's 'best,'" Frank said, standing. "It's wrong."

"You want to be the one to tell the whole town?"

"Yes." Frank turned away.

Fenton Dixon grabbed his son and pulled him close; the old man's breath was hot on Frank's face. "Will you have your own mother disgraced by this news you're so anxious to spread?"

"This isn't about her."

"Yes, it is. And it's about you too, son. It's about all of us."

"Except Joe," Frank said.

"No, I'm thinking of him too. This is what he'd want us to do, wherever he might be."

"But Joe would never . . ." Frank stopped. The truth was, he didn't know anymore what Joe might or might not do. Once, he thought knew.

"Don't get me wrong, son," Fenton said. "I'm happy to learn that Joe may be alive. It's just that he can't come home again, regardless."

"But the truth . . ." Frank started.

Fenton interrupted, "Don't you think Joe would want his name to be spoken around here with respect?"

"You mean your name," Frank said.

"I mean our name."

"And the memorial service tomorrow?" Laura asked.

"Joe was a good boy," Fenton answered. "Why shouldn't the town gather to remember him?"

Frank shook his head.

"You'll do as I say, son."

The next morning, Frank dressed before sunrise. He crept down the stairs and into the parlor, where his father had filled a small box no larger than an ostrich egg with some of Joe's personal possessions (his penknife, his Boy

12

Scout pins, his favorite marbles, two folded newspaper photographs of Tom Mix and William S. Hart, and his tobacco cards, featuring Grover Cleveland Alexander and Walter Johnson). The box was placed on a long table draped in black crepe. It was to be buried later that morning after the memorial service—buried in place of the "fallen" flyer.

Three years before, Frank himself had nearly been buried. Joe had saved him.

It happened like this: Frank was hiking on the rocky ground outside the Cavendish Caves. He and Joe had separated a quarter-mile back. Near the entrance to the largest cave, Frank stepped into a muddy puddle that concealed a crust of earth worn thin. The ground broke beneath his foot, and with a shout he slipped in a rain of mud into a dark chamber below. The fall knocked him unconscious. When he awoke it was night. The concussion confused his senses and clouded his memory. No sight, no sound, only the scent of damp earth everywhere. He thought he was dead. In all, he was alone for just over two hours, though he could not have said if it was hours or days or some terrible measurement outside of time altogether. Then he heard Joe's voice calling his name. Still, he did not believe that he was alive until Joe shined his electric torch down into the hole, then up onto his own grinning face, leaning through the opening. "What are you doing down there?"

"Where am I?" Frank called up.

"Halfway to Hell," Joe said, laughing. "You okay?"

"I guess so."

"I'll get a rope and be right back. You sure you're okay?"

Frank would participate in no mock burial of his still-living brother.

He grabbed the box from the crepe-draped table and moved out onto the porch, closing the door quietly behind him. The first light hinted in the east. He rolled his Indian V-twin out from the shed, first securing the box in one of the bike's saddlebags. Before starting his motorcycle's engine he pushed the bike up the road, past the Parker place and almost to the ice house, so as not to alert his mother and father to his leaving. The smell of gasoline cut through the morning. He was glad that for a few minutes all he would see of the world was the narrow swath made visible by his headlight. He wished everything could be reduced to what lay directly ahead—nothing behind, nothing to the sides. For this, the Old Mill Road seemed best; it was long, winding, and fast. He took his goggles from where they hung on the handlebars and adjusted them on his head.

Then he screamed out of Bayport.

Now, standing atop the promontory at the end of the Old Mill Road, gazing down on the awakening town, Frank spoke to his absent brother. "The last time we were together in this place you said, 'If you were me, Frank, what would you do?' And I didn't answer because I wanted you to think I was as brave as the next guy. But I wish I had answered you, Joe. Because if I'd been honest I'd have said: 'I'd stay with you, Joe. I wouldn't go away because you're my brother and it isn't worth going anyplace without you. Not even to war.'"

Silence.

"Maybe if I'd said that you would have stayed, Joe. Probably not. Either way I wish I'd said it."

More silence.

"Kid brothers don't go off to war by themselves. I know that. I should have been there with you, Joe. We're a team, right? But they said I was unfit to serve. Can you forgive me?"

Nothing.

"Where are you, Joe? Where are we? The Dixon boys."

Then Frank remembered—he was a detective, as his brother had been.

And now Joe was a missing person.

Frank did not return home but rode his motorcycle away.

Another Disappearance

Presently, as Nancy Drew drove into a clearing,
she was astonished to see how dark it had
become.

Carolyn Keene
The Secret of the Old Clock

One week short of graduating as valedictorian of River Heights High School, class of 1921, Carolyn Keene unstrapped a suitcase from the back of her blue roadster, which she had parked in a gravel lot across from the train station. She lifted down the bag; it was heavy, but she didn't mind. Carolyn believed in doing things for herself, even on this most difficult morning of her life. Particularly on this most difficult morning.

"Please, Miss, let me help you," a porter called. He had been standing outside the otherwise deserted station. The building was the town's grandest, though no more than ten or twelve passenger trains passed through on any single day. Now, the porter moved toward her, his gait arthritic, but rapid. Carolyn picked up the bag and started toward the station.

"Let me take that bag for you, Miss."

"Thank you, but I can carry it," Carolyn said, continuing toward the depot.

The porter stepped in front of her. "Oh no, Miss. I need to help you."

She stopped.

Carolyn's body was long and narrow. Nonetheless, she was strong. For the past five years—that is, since about the time of her mother's death—she had risen each day at sunrise and walked all the way to the county road, rain or shine, before returning home to prepare coffee and breakfast for her father, Carson, an attorney whose sedentary lifestyle sometimes worried young Carolyn. For such a girl, carrying a suitcase filled with undergarments and dresses was nothing much. But Carolyn knew the porter's insistence had little to do with strength. She knew it was about doing yet another ordinary thing in the prescribed fashion. Carolyn was better than most at fulfilling such expectations. Everyone in town recognized her social graces. But on this morning—as she considered what might lie beyond the distant, frightening point where the railroad tracks vanished into the horizon—she wondered if these prescriptions were as benevolent as she had always assumed.

"It's my job," the porter continued.

She set the bag on the ground.

The porter picked it up.

"Wait," she said.

He turned to her. "What is it, Miss?"

"How old are you?"

"Seventy-seven, Miss."

"I should be carrying bags for you, if you really think about it."

He laughed. "That's very funny, Miss."

"I don't mean to be funny."

One of the things Carolyn appreciated most about her father was that he never laughed at her ideas, however unusual they might seem to others. Even when Carolyn was a child, Carson Keene spoke to her just as he'd have spoken to a peer—or so it seemed to her at the time. His manner was formal, but not cold. Rather, his warmth seemed to come from his head as well as his heart. Carolyn believed this made his love reliable. She could not imagine ever trusting an affection less grounded than that affection she had come to know in her father's home. That is, their home, Carson and Carolyn's.

"I like a good sense of humor in a young woman," the porter said. "In anybody, for that matter. Especially this early in the morning. Starts the day just right. Like a hot cup of coffee."

Carolyn's mother had been different from Carson. She was more boisterous and demonstrative. Neighbors suggested that these characteristics were a powerful attraction to the young Carson. Carolyn too had loved the sound of her mother's laughter in the house; sometimes, however, the laughter seemed directed at little Carolyn, whose temper was touched off by nothing so quickly as the hint of ridicule. Nonetheless, her mother's lullabies and tender hands managed always to soothe her. Carolyn remembered her mother's tears too, which she had come to believe were inevitable in the life of one who lives so much by her heart. Shortly after her mother's funeral, during which thirteen-year-old Carolyn collapsed in her father's arms, she resolved that there would be no more tears in her father's house. This, she had accomplished.

Until last night.

"Why is my carrying my own suitcase so funny, exactly?"

His smile remained broad. "Well, it's just not your place, Miss. To be carrying anybody's bags."

"But it's your place?"

"Yes, Miss," he answered without hesitation.

"I don't think so," she said.

He stopped, his eyes fixing hers. "Well, maybe that's not for you to say, child."

"Oh." Carolyn's father sometimes counseled her against arrogance, which he warned her could grow like a weed from the otherwise well-tended soil of self-confidence.

"Besides," the porter added, "somebody might be watching us, Miss. Now, you wouldn't want nobody to see us acting like fools. You carrying your own bag! Me walking alongside, watching you work. It'd get me fired, or worse. Believe me."

He started again for the station.

"Nobody's watching us," Carolyn said. "Nobody's around."

"Somebody's always watching," he answered without breaking stride. "Besides, I'm still good for something. I got to be."

She followed him into the empty station.

"I'm sorry," she said.

"No need."

She tipped him, then watched him disappear into the baggage room.

She stood alone in the depot. Almost two hours remained before the arrival of the first train. Even this room, high and long as a school gymnasium, was not large enough to hold all the things that Carolyn Keene did not know about real life, she thought—regardless of whatever self-confidence she had felt a mere day before. She looked about her. A row of ticket windows, behind which agents would shortly take their places, lined one wall. Above the ticket windows, the train-schedule board, black with white letters now all ajumble, waited to clack and clatter into coherence. At the center of the room, dozens of leather seats were set back to back in two long rows. Carolyn sank into one.

A three-foot-wide wall clock read 6:22.

She had not slept the night before. Hannah had made dinner for Carolyn, Carson, and Anne Talbot, Carson's twenty-six-year-old fiancée who lived, temporarily, in a boardinghouse down the road. Anne had seemed somewhat reserved at dinner. She had expressed none of her familiar dissatisfactions with the provincial characteristics of River Heights. It was true that Anne had grown fond of their housekeeper Hannah's cooking and had some time ago stopped comparing their simple suppers to the sumptuous and sophisticated meals she had enjoyed in Chicago. Still, it remained a rare evening that Anne failed to express dismay at the more significant cultural inadequacies of River Heights and the shallowness of its inhabitants—current company always excepted, of course. Now, sinking deeper into the waiting room chair, Carolyn realized that she might have guessed as early as the soup course that on this night something was different about Anne, her future stepmother. This is what Carolyn knew of how Anne had come into her father's life:

Six months before, at an elegant Oak Park dinner party, Carson Keene had been seated next to Anne, the daughter of one of his most powerful clients. She was lovely in a lavender dress with a camellia pattern, which Anne later described to Carolyn as being "positively antebellum and, therefore, positively *irresistible.*" Anne's dinner conversation had been witty, her background impressive, her eyes hungry, and her lips a subtle shade of red. The night of the social affair, Carolyn herself was far away in River Heights studying for a biology midterm. Her father's business trips always worried Carolyn. At home alone, she fretted about the dangers that lurked out of state. She envisioned train wrecks (which is how she had lost her mother) or late-night stickups. In night-

mares, Carolyn sometimes watched helplessly as her father choked to death on a piece of room-service roast beef in one or another anonymous hotel room. She would awaken from such dreams in a sweat, guilty at her failure to protect him. Until Anne, it had never occurred to Carolyn that something other than business or death could take place on one of her father's trips.

One line in a telegram changed all that—

"Met lovely woman. Proposed marriage. You'll love her."

Anne Talbot carried herself with a confidence and sophistication that both frightened and attracted Carolyn. They were very little alike. Sometimes Carolyn could not understand how her father had become enamored of a woman who was inadequate at so many ordinary things. Anne could not cook, could not sew, could not drive, could not play the piano, could not walk a dog, could not hold babies, could not remember the names of neighbors, could not keep track of her room key at the boardinghouse, and— most decidedly—could not (and would never!) carry her own luggage.

On the other hand, Carolyn had to admit that Anne was graceful in ways no girl from River Heights could ever be. For example, she did not merely speak French—as Carolyn did—but had studied it for two years at the Sorbonne, where among other things she had acquired culinary tastes that now befuddled Louise and Dale at the River Heights Diner. She had met Left Bank painters, hinting that she had once posed nude for one, and regularly peppered her conversations with foreign references that seemed natural coming from her lips. Additionally, her neck was long and her skin was as perfect and white as the surface of a lily. Sometimes, Carolyn wanted to touch that smooth skin with the tips of her fingers. "Of course," she thought, "Father must feel the same way—only more so." Beyond that thought, however, Carolyn dared not venture.

"What a lovely girl!" Anne had exclaimed when she met Carolyn. "We're going to be such great friends!"

They were not great friends.

Carolyn knew that her father was unhappy that his "two girls" were not closer. Of late, on those rare occasions when Anne was absent at a meal, the conversation between father and daughter consisted of Carson's listing ways in which Carolyn might make Anne feel more at home in River Heights.

"She really likes you, Carolyn," Carson would explain.

Carolyn believed otherwise—sure, Anne acted friendly enough, but Carolyn could not miss the criticisms implicit in Anne's regular suggestions regarding the domestic life Carolyn and her father had happily shared for so many years. For example: Shouldn't the furniture in the parlor be rearranged? Or: Isn't the artwork on the walls somewhat unsophisticated for a successful attorney's household? Mightn't a new, more accomplished set of friends enliven the Keenes' otherwise *rather provincial* social life? Wouldn't Carson look younger in a more fashionable wardrobe? "All just friendly suggestions, of course," Anne explained. More like an armed invasion, Carolyn thought. But she did not have the heart to confess her antipathy toward Anne to her father, who seemed happier—despite everything—since Anne had entered their lives. "Oh, yes, I like her too, Dad," Carolyn would answer.

"Anne and I only want the best for you," he'd continue. "Now that you're pretty much, well, grown up."

"Oh, I know that."

On the night before Carolyn arrived at the train station, as she climbed into bed and switched off the light on her bedstand, she heard strange sounds coming from down the darkened hallway—from the direction of her father's room. She sat up in bed, listening. Once, she had spent four nights in the home of the Turnbull sisters, whose mansion was said to be haunted. They had called on Carolyn to help them because they knew she was brave and reliable. Screams had emanated from the walls of the Turnbulls' place. Ultimately, Carolyn discovered a secret staircase in the old mansion and unmasked the neighborhood pranksters whose idea of a good time was to frighten two old women. Carolyn's first thought now was that the pranksters had returned, perhaps in vengeance. But the sounds were different. These were not screams, but moans. A woman. Sometimes a man, groaning. Muffled. She went to her door, opened it, and stepped into the darkened hall.

The sounds came from the direction of her father's bedroom. "Dad?" she called.

She heard a voice from within her father's room.

"Shhh . . ." her father whispered to someone.

The moaning stopped.

"Shhh . . . "

Then Anne's whisper: "Oh, Carson. Don't stop."

At last, Carolyn understood.

She slipped back into her room, into her bed, and closed her eyes. How could she be so stupid! she wondered.

A few minutes later, Carolyn's bedroom door opened.

"Dad?" Carolyn whispered.

"No, it's me," Anne answered. "Your father's sleeping."

"I thought you went home," Carolyn said. "You know, hours ago."

"Carolyn, you knew I was still here."

"Yes."

"May I talk to you for a few minutes?"

Carolyn sat up in her bed. "Okay."

Anne stepped into the room. Her clothes were perfect, as if she had not left them in a heap an hour before; her hair showed no sign of tussle. She set her handbag on the bureau and closed the door behind her.

The room was lit only by the moon.

Anne sat on the edge of Carolyn's bed. "I know you don't like me," she whispered.

"That's not true."

"Shhh . . ." Anne interrupted. "It doesn't matter. Not anymore."

"Why?" Carolyn asked.

"I'm going away."

"Well, it's very late. Time to sleep."

"No, I mean forever," Anne said.

"What?"

"Shhh . . ." Anne put her finger to Carolyn's lips. "Your father's sleeping, remember?"

Carolyn nodded.

"Carson loves us both, Carolyn. In different ways, of course. That you and I don't get along exactly as he'd like, well, it's tearing him to pieces. You must see it. The poor man. I know you want the best for him. Same as I do. I'm sure you've been tearing your hair out wondering what you can do to help him."

"But I like you just fine," Carolyn said. "I tell him so all the time."

"Well, 'just fine' is not good enough for your father. You know how he is, Carolyn. You know how perfect he wants everything to be. But we can never be what he wants, not living together I mean, and I can't bear to give him anything short of the perfection he deserves. You must understand, Carolyn."

"Well, I want the best for him."

"Of course you do."

"But you don't have to go away, Anne."

"I do. Our personalities, yours and mine, well . . . The two of us together . . . A little tension . . . It'll eventually destroy your father's faith in family. And you know as well as I do that we can't change simply by willing it. We're too different, you and I. You're wonderful, Carolyn. Still, I'd ask you to change if I believed you could. Or I'd change myself if I could. But people can't change. Maybe you don't know that, Carolyn, but my years have shown me. It's sad but true. I have to leave your father so he can keep his faith. It'll hurt him, deeply, but I'm sure having you around will soothe his pain."

"Me? No, Anne."

"You can be his treasure, forever."

His treasure—yes, Carolyn thought. But forever?

"You're such a good girl, Carolyn. You always do the right thing."

"No, Anne."

"Shhh . . . Don't worry about me, Carolyn. The world's a marvelous place. Why, if I were a few years younger, I'd look on leaving here as a wonderful adventure. I'm not a girl anymore, Carolyn. But don't worry, I'll be all right. I only want you to think of the pain this spares your father."

"But I like you just fine, Anne. I think you're amazing, in a way."

Anne looked at Carolyn. "'Amazing'? That's quite a versatile word."

"Look, don't leave him for my sake."

"I never said it was for your sake, but his."

"He wants you, Anne. It'll work out."

"Carolyn, consider for once that you might not know everything."

"I know I don't know everything."

"Just consider your poor father."

"But he doesn't want you to go," Carolyn answered, straining to keep her voice to a whisper.

"True, Carolyn. But we're women. When it comes to matters of the heart, we know best. His future happiness is in our hands."

"But . . ."

Anne put her index finger once more to Carolyn's lips. "I know your intentions are good." Then she moved her hand to Carolyn's cheek. "I know you love your father, but you have to trust me. You're such a good girl, Carolyn."

"No, not really."

"I wish I was like you, Carolyn."

"No you don't," she answered, pulling away.

Anne smiled. "So strong and resolute."

"Why are you telling me this? If you're going to go, go. Why have you brought me into this? Couldn't you have just disappeared? Why do I have to be a . . ." She searched for the word. "A conspirator."

"This is about kindness, not secrecy."

"Then why isn't Dad here?"

"Do you want me to call him?" Anne asked. "Do you want me to explain to him why I'm leaving?"

"Well, no."

"Then you're a conspirator, my dear girl."

"I'm not your girl."

"Oh, of course. I'm sorry."

Despite everything, Anne looked beautiful—her eyes wide and blue, her skin white, her lips red. Mary Pickford was not more beautiful, Carolyn thought. She suspected it would never matter to her father if Anne learned to drive or cook or shop or play the piano. All that would ever matter was that Anne's imported perfume smell of white flowers afloat on a rolling sea and that her skin feel as warm and smooth and rich as Carolyn imagined it must.

"You and I are partners," Anne said.

"How's that?"

"We love the same man."

Carolyn shrugged. "In different ways, I guess."

Anne crossed the room to her handbag, from which she removed an envelope. Then she turned back to the girl. "I want you to keep this," she said, returning to the edge of the bed. "It's a list of my friends in Paris. When I was about your age, studying at the Sorbonne, they took me in with such warmth and generosity that I feel blessed even to this day. They'd take care of you too, incidentally. Which I mention just to give you some idea of their generosity. They'll always know how to reach me, wherever I end up. Someday, drop me a line to tell me how your father's life is turning out."

"Anne, I can't let you do this."

Anne placed the envelope on the bed beside her.

"I'm leaving the day after tomorrow," Anne said. "The Denver Behemoth to Detroit, then on to New York, and then, who knows? I don't plan to discuss this with your father. Words would only bring him more pain, which is the last thing you or I want for that man, right?"

"But . . ."

Anne stopped her. "There's no sense discussing a decision that's already been made, Carolyn. It's best just to leave a note behind and then be gone. It's much kinder. Life is like this. Don't worry, he won't blame you for my disappearance. He's much too big a man to do that, don't you think?"

Anne stood. She started for the door.

"Blame me?" Carolyn said. Everything was moving so fast.

Anne opened the door to go.

"Wait. He doesn't *want* this," Carolyn managed to say.

"You're right," Anne answered. "But I don't know any other way to spare him."

Then Anne was gone. The house was silent.

Now, Carolyn Keene sat in a leather chair at the center of the awakening train station. Of course, there was an alternative to Anne's leaving. Carolyn had packed her two suitcases in the dark. She had rolled her roadster halfway down Maple Street before starting its engine so as not to awaken her father. Her plan was that he would find her note, which she had left on her bureau, long after the Denver Behemoth had whisked Carolyn (and the conflict that was cleaving his heart) out of town. He would have no opportunity to stop her, whatever his inclination. Or so Carolyn hoped.

Or did not hope.

She too was conflicted.

The truth was, with each action she had undertaken to conceal her motives and destination—including the note in which she claimed to be leaving home to fulfill a life-long desire to "see the world"—she found herself hoping that her father would see through the concealment and at the last minute arrive at the station to stop her from carrying out her selfless plan. Carson was a bright man, she reminded herself. The best attorney in town. Their town. Carolyn loved River Heights. This was where she was *Carolyn Keene*, the bright, strong young woman with a whole life before her— who would she ever be elsewhere?

It was 8:23.

Nearly fifty minutes remained before the Behemoth arrived. Plenty of time. Dozens of travelers—alone, in pairs, or as whole families—entered the increasingly noisy station.

Now, Carolyn was just one of many sitting in the waiting room. She looked at each traveler, disappointed that none were Carson Keene. Still, when she actually saw him walk into the station—a look of worry etched on his face—she thought at first that he must be a hallucination, born of sleeplessness and fear. It was not until he spoke that she realized he had really come for her.

"Carolyn, my girl," he said.

She jumped out of her seat.

He wrapped her in his arms.

"How did you know I was here?" she asked.

"Where else would you go to begin 'seeing the world'?"

She smiled. "I should have known I'd never fool you."

"Let's sit down, Carolyn."

They sat.

"Tell me, why did you want to leave . . ."

"Oh, I don't know," she interrupted.

". . . without first saying good-bye?" Carson finished.

"What?"

"Sure, you should have said something."

"Oh, well, I thought it would be less painful."

"Painful?"

"And I didn't want you trying to talk me out of it, Dad."

"Why would I do that, Carolyn?"

Carolyn did not know what to say. Too many answers to Carson's question came at once to her mind: Perhaps because you love me and need me and can't really imagine your life without me in it, she thought. Perhaps because I love you and need you and can't really imagine my life without you in it. And other good answers too. So many that she was left now with a question of her own: How could Carson Keene not already know all these answers?

"Travel is good," Carson said, handing her an envelope. "You're a bright, brave girl, just as I raised you to be. Nothing out there will ever be too much for you to handle."

"I thought you might be upset about my missing graduation," she suggested.

He shook his head. "Don't worry, we'll mail your diploma wherever you go. There's no reason for you to delay your plans. I'm very proud of you, Carolyn. Being valedictorian is not really about making a speech; it's about learning, which you've already accomplished. The rest is just ceremony."

She noticed a line of sweat at his scalp where his hair was growing thin.

"What's in the envelope?" she asked.

"Oh, it's that list of Anne's friends in Paris. You left it on the bureau beside your note. You might make use of it sometime. I'm sure they're interesting people. And there's something else in there too. Look."

She opened the envelope. A check. "Two thousand dollars?"

He nodded.

"Dad, I have my own account, you know."

"Sure, but think of this as a graduation present. And a ticket to anywhere in the world."

She said nothing.

"Don't I get a hug?" he asked.

She leaned forward and put her arms around her father.

"Oh, Carolyn, my girl."

When she pulled away, she noticed tears in his eyes.

"Dad?"

"Yes."

"Do you *want* me to go?"

"Of course not, Carolyn. But our lives . . . sometimes they're not all ours."

"What does that mean?"

He shrugged. "Complications, conflict. Time works all things out."

"You mean Anne?"

"Oh no, you mustn't blame Anne."

"Then what are you talking about?"

"Oh, nothing, Carolyn. I'm just happy for you to see the world. Your adventurous spirit is admirable. Didn't you always say you wanted to travel?"

"Why are you talking to me like this, Dad?"

"Like what?"

"Like a stranger."

"Oh, come now."

"A frightened stranger."

"Well, my little girl's leaving home. Shouldn't I be a little worried?"

"As a matter of fact, yes."

"See?"

"But that's not it, Dad. This is nothing like when you used to see me off to summer camp. I mean, you'd be worried, but you were still you. And I was still me. And we were still us."

"Yeah."

"But it's different now."

"We all make mistakes, Carolyn."

"If you're about to make a mistake with your life, then stop. Today."

"Oh, if a mistake's been made, it's one I made long ago."

"What does that mean?"

His eyes welled with tears. "Life is so damn complicated," he said, standing. "I can't even begin to tell you."

"I don't understand."

"Maybe that's better." He turned away.

"Won't you wait with me until the train comes?"

"I can't."

"Why not?"

Then he was gone.

Outside on the platform, as the Denver Behemoth pulled into the station, Carolyn discovered herself standing beside the old porter. The morning had gotten busy for him; nonetheless, he stopped beside Carolyn.

"Hello, Miss," he said.

Ordinarily, she'd have simply nodded. But not today. She discovered herself drawn to the old man, whose name she did not know. He had at least dared to contradict her, she thought. *Well, maybe that's not for you to say, child.* In his recrimination, there had seemed more real connection than in most words of praise Carolyn had received from the faculty and class at River Heights High. Now, he smiled at her as if he did not hate her, despite her faults.

"Have a good trip, Miss," he said.

Foremost among her faults, she thought, was the bitterest ignorance. For example, how had her father learned about Anne's list of Parisian acquaintances? she wondered. She did not want to speculate, but turned to the porter. "Tell me, what happens to love?" she asked.

"What, Miss?"

"When love goes, where does it go?"

He looked confused.

"I mean, nothing just disappears, does it?" she asked.

"That's a mystery, Miss." Then he nodded. "Maybe if you were some kind of detective, well, maybe you could solve it."

"All aboard!" called the conductor from up the line.

A Stolen Suitcase, 1923

*Frank groped about among the rubbish in one corner
until at last he rose with an exclamation of triumph,
holding aloft a shining object.*

Franklin W. Dixon
The Tower Treasure

Frank Dixon stood in the Louvre museum among a tour group of Ohioans who pressed together on a wide marble staircase that led up from the foyer to the winged statue, *Victory of Samothrace*. Members of the group strained to catch the accented words of their guide, who gestured toward the massive sculpture: "Isn't she a fine example of Hellenistic art?"

"She's lovely," a matronly woman whispered to Frank. "Even headless."

As yet, no one had noticed that Frank wore no beribboned nametag; he was not a member of this group, the Dayton Chamber of Commerce Travel and Adventure Society.

"Oh, yes, lovely," he said.

Frank preferred to meet his informants in places like this—crowded, public places anywhere off the Left Bank, which teemed with too many of his own curious neighbors. Like any private investigator, he required anonymity, which was difficult for an American to achieve in a foreign city— even a city overrun with Americans. The company of tourists offered the best cover. Now, Frank glanced about the rotunda below. He saw no one suspicious. However, in eighteen months of private investigations he had learned that it was rarely the "suspicious types" one needed to watch for. The dark villain of Conan Doyle's misty London was primarily a creature of fiction. Rather, the embezzlers, blackmailers, runaways, and adulterers that Frank pursued tried to blend into crowds—much like Frank himself, who pressed now with the rest of his tour group past the "Winged Victory" and toward the Renaissance paintings. He hoped to find more than a mere smile waiting for him at the Mona Lisa. It was his rendezvous point with the mysterious woman named Alice, whose note that morning had been so rich with the promise of information, Frank's stock in trade.

Frank pressed into the center of the group.

A mustachioed, city-councilman type turned to him with a look of consternation when their shoulders brushed in the hall between paintings by Giotto and Fra Angelico. "Hey, you're not from Dayton," he observed.

"You're right," Frank said. "Do you think we might keep that between you and me?"

"But you're not part of our group!"

"Okay, okay." He handed the councilman a business card. "I'm a private investigator working to recover stolen property."

The councilman studied the card, then nodded and winked as he slipped it into his pocket. "I see. Are you tracking down a stolen painting?"

Frank shook his head. "A suitcase filled with short stories."

"Stories? Why would anybody steal something like that?" the councilman asked. "I mean, where's the value?"

Frank knew the value of short stories. He had always been an appreciative reader; however, it was his frustrated efforts these past months to write a short story of his own that taught him their true cost. He did not aspire to be a professional writer. Even so, he had been a spinner of yarns since his school days when he assigned adventurous purposes to the custom-made shoe he was forced to wear on his bad leg (claiming, for example, that the thick rubber sole was hollow and contained secret government documents or nitroglycerin that would explode if he stamped his foot). Starting to write a short story was easy, he discovered. Who among those living on the Left Bank was not engaged in some sort of artistic enterprise? But finishing a short story . . .

Impossible, so far. At least for Frank. "Are you holding out on me?" the councilman asked, tapping with his finger at Frank's lapel in the crowded Louvre hallway. "There's something about that suitcase you're not telling me. I'm no rube. There's something valuable that's been sewn into the lining of the suitcase, right?"

"Not that I know of."

"Something like jewels or opium!"

"No, it's just short stories," Frank said.

Frank had befriended a Belgian émigré named Georges Simenon who wrote potboiler novels at a rate of one a month. Simenon advised Frank on writing fiction. Begin with a compelling character in an intriguing situation, he suggested. Frank had attempted to follow his friend's formula. His first story began with a blind maharaja lost overnight in an Indian jungle; his second story began with a pirate trying to remember where he had buried his treasure; his third story began with a jazz trumpeter attempting to solve a crime while aboard a whaling ship in the Arctic. However, Frank abandoned each of the stories after becoming hopelessly entangled in the threads of their plots.

Unfinished, unfinished, unfinished . . .

But he did not lose sleep over his writing.

Rather, he lost sleep over his true vocation, which was likewise unfinished—after all these years he had not yet located his brother, Joe.

"Why would somebody pay good money to recover something like a bunch of stories?" the councilman continued.

"Well . . . " Frank started.

But the councilman did not wait for an answer; he turned away from Frank toward a wall-sized painting of carnage and nudity.

Frank was glad not to have to explain.

The week before, an American woman named Hadley Hemingway had burst into Frank's office. She cared very much about such a suitcase, which she had recently lost at the Gare de Lyon before boarding a train to Switzerland to join her husband, a hopeful young writer who she claimed would one day be the most famous in the world (one of how many thousand around Montparnasse? Frank had thought). The man's name was Ernest and all of his writings had been inside the lost suitcase. "Please, Mr. Dixon, you must help me!" she pleaded as she settled into a wooden chair beside Frank's desk.

"Of course," he answered. "But please call me Frank."

She nodded and took a deep breath.

Frank's office consisted of a single, dimly lit attic room five stories above the Boulevard du Montparnasse. On the directory downstairs:

Franklin Dixon
Investigateur Privé
Les Disparus, etc.
5A

The room's ceiling sloped down at a steep angle from the interior wall to a gabled window through which Frank had spent more hours than he cared to consider watching men in straw boaters and women in all manner of sleek chapeaux moving up and down the boulevard. They had a vitality in their step that he feared his own movements were coming to lack. Work was sporadic at best for an American private investigator in Paris. The desk and chair took up most of the attic room, leaving space only in one corner for a filing cabinet and in another for a large antique globe that Frank had bought at a flea market shortly after his arrival in Paris. On the wall behind the desk hung a framed photograph of Joe, whom Frank described to clients as his partner—even though Frank had heard nothing from Joe since his disappearance in 1918 and had been unable to locate him in the eighteen months since he'd opened his P.I. practice here.

"Can you help me?" Mrs. Hemingway asked.

"You've come to the right place, Ma'am."

She was a clear-eyed woman—five or more years older than Frank—and wore drab, baggy clothing and shoes worn down to their last eighth-inch of leather. Another client with no money, Frank thought. Nonetheless, he was glad she had come. Her hair was trimmed short and her body was strong and thick but very feminine. Frank liked her from the moment he saw her. She looked like a woman one could trust (except with luggage), which made this Ernest fellow luckier than he probably knew. The streets were full of glamorous types. Frank himself had known a few this past year. Here was a woman to keep a man warm, he thought. And safe.

"Your husband kept no carbon copies of his work?" he asked.

She shook her head. "I've lost his life's work!"

"Why were you taking the suitcase to Switzerland?"

"Ernest had gone on ahead, on a skiing holiday," she explained. "I thought I'd surprise him with his typewriter and all of his drafts. That way when the weather was bad he could stay inside and write. He loves to work. He's very good."

"Does your husband have a mustache?" Frank asked.

"Yes, why?"

"I think I've seen him here and there. They call him 'Hem'?"

"Yes, everyone knows him."

"He seems like a good fellow."

"Oh, he's a dear, but he's so . . . serious about his fiction. He sends dispatches to newspapers in Kansas City and Toronto. But journalism means nothing to him. His fiction is everything. He's doing very exciting new things. At least he was. Now, he's so beside himself with grief that he's not writing at all. I'm so afraid he'll never forgive me, Mr. Dixon. And all I wanted to do was surprise him."

"Well, I'm sure you've surprised him, Mrs. Hemingway."

"He's such a dear; he hasn't spoken a cross word to me, Mr. Dixon."

"That's good."

"No, it's not good. He hasn't spoken to me at all."

"I'm sorry."

She wiped a tear from her eye.

"How exactly did you lose the suitcase?" Frank asked.

"I just set it down on the platform between tracks seven and eight. I turned my head for one moment, and it was gone. Is it foolish of me to think there's any chance you might find it?"

"When was it stolen?"

"Six days ago."

Slim chance, Frank thought.

Now it had been five days since Hadley Hemingway's visit, and in that time Frank had made more progress in pursuit of the stolen suitcase than he'd thought likely. He had learned that good investigative work consisted first of nurturing a willingness to sit for long hours outside buildings, taking note of whoever did or did not walk in and out and, second, of developing a network of contacts who, through their own networks, were connected with a geometrically increasing number of informants until a report of almost anything that occurred anywhere in the city became obtainable for a few well-placed francs. Frank began his search for the stolen suitcase at the Gare de Lyon, where his friend André waited on tables outside the *brasserie* near platforms eight and nine and noted on his pad, beside orders of pastries, *croque-monsieur,* and café au lait, any suspicious activities he observed among the travelers. André had not witnessed the theft; however, for a few francs he suggested Frank talk to a man called L'Ecureuil, the Squirrel, who pinched more luggage from the Gare de Lyon than any of the other thieves who came through the station.

Frank took the Métro to Montmartre.

L'Ecureuil sat in a dark corner of the bar at the Hôtel Le Bouquet. He sipped an anisette and indicated with a slicing

39

motion of his hand that Frank should join him. Frank sat, slipping a fifty-franc note across the table as he explained his situation to L'Ecureuil, who answered that he had indeed stolen such a suitcase as Frank described. Frank slipped another fifty across the table and L'Ecureuil explained that he had been hired to steal that specific suitcase by a mild, middle-aged woman named Alice who had learned of L'Ecureuil's special skills through his brother-in-law, a talkative baker with a thriving business near the Luxembourg Gardens. L'Ecureuil did not know Alice's last name, nor had he opened the suitcase to examine its contents before delivering it to her in a taxi outside the Gare de Lyon three minutes after the theft. He did not reveal the terms of his agreement with Alice but suggested that for fifty francs more he would tell Frank the name of his baker brother-in-law, who surely knew where Alice lived.

Fifty francs more.

The bakery was mere blocks from Frank's office. However, the brother-in-law baker was unwilling to supply Frank with the information he sought, regardless of the fifty-franc notes piling up on his butter-slick counter. For all of Frank's reassurances, the baker never seemed to trust that he was not an undercover policeman, hot on the heels of this flour-bedecked conspirator. At last, the baker agreed to take a note from Frank to deliver to Alice the next time she came into the shop.

Three weeks later, a note arrived at Frank's flat:

Dear Sir,
I understand you have a question for me about a missing suitcase. I'm afraid I am not one to keep malicious secrets, despite the urging of my beloved,

and so I feel compelled to make your acquaintance.
Please meet me at the portrait of Lisa del Giocondo
tomorrow at noon.
Sincerely,
Alice B. Toklas

Now the tour guide pulled together the members of the
Dayton Chamber of Commerce Travel and Adventure Society
in the crowded gallery before the most famous painting in
the world. He raised his hand above his head to call for their
attention. "The 'Mona Lisa,' also known as the portrait of
Lisa del Giocondo or, simply, 'La Gioconda,' was painted by
Leonardo da Vinci in the first decade of the sixteenth century,"
he said. "It demonstrates with utmost brilliance many
aspects of Florentine and Umbrian portraiture. . . ."

But Frank had not come here for an art lecture.

"Mr. Dixon?"

He turned. A small, dark woman indicated with a shrug
of her shoulder that he was to follow her out of the crowd of
Ohioans. They moved without speaking down the hall of Renaissance masterpieces, turned down the stairs near the *Victory
of Samothrace,* passed through the foyer, and finally
stopped in the courtyard outside the museum entrance. She
turned to him, extending her hand.

"I'm Alice Toklas."

"I'm Frank Dixon," he said, shaking her hand. She was
perhaps forty years old. Her American English was touched
by a slight western accent. Perhaps California. She carried a
handbag out of which protruded a skein of knitting yarn and
two needles. Very domesticated. She was not what Frank
had expected. "Thank you for coming, Miss Toklas."

"Well, I fear a wrong has been committed."

"Thank you for your conscience."

"Yes, well . . ." She stopped.

"Do you have the suitcase?" he asked.

"Not exactly," she answered.

"But you know where it is?"

"Yes."

He reached into his pocket.

She stopped him. "Please," she said. "This isn't about money."

"Oh? What's it about?"

"Art."

"I don't understand."

"Well, the suitcase was not stolen as a mere piece of luggage."

"You're referring to the short stories and the novel?"

"Of course."

"They're extremely valuable?" Frank asked.

She shook her head. "They're utterly worthless."

"I don't understand."

"Pay a visit to my friend and me tonight. For apéritifs, around nine. She'll explain it all to you. She understands so much."

Alice Toklas turned and started away.

"Where will I find you?" Frank called.

"Oh, of course." She stopped and turned back, handing to Frank an engraved note card that read:

Gertrude Stein
27 Rue de Fleurus
Paris

"Good-bye, Mr. Dixon," Alice said.

The name Gertrude Stein was familiar to Frank. He had heard it spoken from time to time in the Latin Quarter by artists and writers and the most culturally ambitious new wave of American tourists. Miss Stein was known for her good taste in art, her intelligent conversation, and her indecipherable prose and poetry.

At nine o'clock Frank knocked at the door of twenty-seven Rue de Fleurus.

Miss Stein, a short, powerfully built woman with sharp eyes, answered the door, extended her hand for a firm shake, and admitted Frank to a large salon. There, the walls all the way up to the ten-foot-high ceiling were hung with paintings that took Frank's breath away. He had seen nothing like it—not even in the Musée de Luxembourg, where he liked to stroll on afternoons. Here was Picasso, Matisse, Gris.

"All of them friends of mine," Miss Stein said.

"Very impressive."

"Just paint on canvas," she answered. "But generally well accomplished. As for the artists themselves, well, some are more impressive than others, believe me. As gentlemen, as men in general. Perhaps one day I'll introduce you to some of them, if you're interested in such things."

"Of course," Frank answered. How could one live in this city for two years and not be interested? "It's a pleasure to make your acquaintance, Miss Stein," he continued. "I've heard your name spoken quite often with great respect in cafés and galleries."

She nodded. "I have lived in this city for nineteen years now, Mr. Dixon. In that time, a little whispered respect among drunken artists and writers is not so much to have gathered for oneself. Not after the sweat that has gone into my various endeavors."

He looked once more at the paintings. "You seem to have gathered more than mere respect, Miss Stein."

"Oh, the pictures. Yes. Well, do you see the way I am dressed?"

He nodded. "Very nice."

"Very simply," she corrected. "Like a peasant woman, really. But that's how it's always been for me—money enough for either clothes or art. You can see where my priorities lie."

"A very economical exchange," he said.

"Fortunately I have never had to choose between food and art," she continued. "Otherwise, you'd be meeting a severely undernourished woman."

He laughed.

"Of course, friendship has counted for something in my collection as well," she conceded. "Along with my having the most discerning eye for talent in, well, the entire Western world."

Frank smiled. She was not joking.

"Now please follow me, Mr. Dixon."

She led him further into the apartment, where Alice Toklas sat on a sofa working on a needlepoint image of an idyllic country scene. Alice nodded to Frank, then returned her attention to her work. Miss Stein led Frank past her companion and into the dining room, which was walled with books. On the doors were tacked three drawings each by Cézanne and Renoir.

"Please, sit down, Mr. Dixon."

He sat.

"What will you have to drink?" she asked.

"A brandy would be nice."

She turned to a sideboard, taking a bottle from a shelf.

"May I assume you intend to start collecting original manuscripts now as well?" he asked.

"Surely not." She handed him the drink.

"But this matter of the suitcase . . ."

"Please," she interrupted, sitting beside him. "You have an intelligent face, young man. Not incapable of learning a thing or two, I'd imagine. And willing to learn too, right? Your profession would suggest as much."

"I'm always willing to learn."

"Then let me explain something about collecting art that you don't seem to understand."

"All right."

"The most important aim for any collector is to collect work that is actually good," she said.

"And the writing in the suitcase?"

"Not good."

"No?"

She shook her head. "This Hemingway chap is a friend of mine. Have you met him?"

"No, but I've met his wife."

"Well, he's a fine young man, and I believe wholeheartedly in his potential as a writer."

"Then why sabotage his career?"

"I'm not sabotaging it, my dear Mr. Dixon. I'm saving it."

"I don't understand."

"Hemingway is ruthless and headstrong. Now, ruthless-ness can be quite a good thing for a writer. What else is there, really? Compliant? Impossible. Who would ever be interested in the work of a compliant writer? Would you, Mr. Dixon?"

"No."

"But headstrong is not a good thing," she continued. "At least not when it comes to taking criticism, my criticism, that is. You see, Mr. Hemingway visits me often. He flatters and smiles that disarming smile, and I allow him to believe that I am actually flattered and disarmed. But I am really only entertained, which of course is not an insubstantial thing. He is young . . . he's not hard to manage . . . he is like a dozen other young writers and artists who visit me . . . except for one thing—he has real talent. With all these pictures on the walls you may think that talent is a common thing. But believe me, it is more rare than radium. Nonetheless, he doesn't understand that his writing is inaccrochable."

"Inaccrochable?" Frank asked.

"His subject matter, his language . . . unpublishable back in the States. But I believe in Hemingway, Mr. Dixon. More than anyone else in the world believes in him, except perhaps for his dear little wife, who is not really qualified to believe one way or the other in matters of such delicacy. Yes, Hemingway could be great. But that suitcase full of early work has been like an albatross around his neck. He bears it, bears it, bears it. I have simply liberated him of the weighty bird."

"By stealing it?"

She nodded. "One day he will deny and betray me," she continued. "But that is no concern of mine. I am not engaged in this endeavor for gratitude, and he is not capable of it. So we're a perfect match, Hemingway and I."

"Then what are you in this for?" Frank asked.

"Art." She shrugged. "For all my experimentation, I am really somewhat old-fashioned."

"Then you're being quite a good friend to him," Frank said.

"Better than he knows."

"But what of Mrs. Hemingway, who is tortured by the idea that she has lost her husband's work?"

Miss Stein nodded and looked away. "Yes, that's sad. She's a good girl, but he'll be rid of her soon enough. He may not know that yet himself, but . . . art is nothing if not a dirty business, my boy. But what greater end ever justified a means?"

"Love?"

"Ah, perhaps. But good art is always the product of love. Not in obvious ways, perhaps. But love nevertheless. Do you think Picasso does not love his paintings as he's painting them, regardless of what he might say after they're finished? And, sadly, not all loves, the Hemingways' included, ever achieve such heights. Do you understand?"

"I'm not sure."

"One moment, please," she said, before disappearing into another room.

Frank stood and paced about the dining room. He wondered how Miss Stein would feel about the righteousness of stealing if he were to fold and slip one of her Renoir drawings into his jacket pocket. (How fine any of them would look on the wall above his bed!) However, he knew he could never justify his theft as eloquently as Miss Stein had justified hers. Perhaps, he thought, because her theft had really been undertaken with the best intentions. Two years of tracking runaways and photographing adulterers had taught him not to put trust in a black-or-white vision of human endeavors. Miss Stein did have an eye for art—perhaps her views on this young writer's career were equally valid.

"Mr. Dixon?"

He turned. Miss Stein stood in the doorway, a small, battered suitcase in hand. "Of course, I cannot deny you what you've come for," she said. She lifted the suitcase onto the dining table where it settled with a bang. "I am not ruthless, Mr. Dixon. Perhaps that is why I am not more famous at this point in my life than I am. If poor Hadley is so anxious to have all this apprentice work back for her hopelessly strong-willed husband that she would hire a private investigator . . . well, I am not a cruel woman."

Frank opened the suitcase. It was stuffed with manuscripts, some handwritten on lined pages, others typed. He leafed through the stories on top. Their titles: "Old Man," "The Doctor and His Dog," and "The Trouble with People."

"Please keep in mind that my intentions were noble," Miss Stein said. "Also, do not assume that because I have returned the suitcase I have changed my mind about Mr. Hemingway's work or the best direction he might choose for his future. I am merely acquiescing to the momentum of . . . sentimentality."

"I wasn't hired to reveal the name of the thief, Miss Stein. Only to recover the suitcase."

"Thief?" she answered, smiling. "How exciting!"

"Please, I mean no offense," Frank said.

"Oh, none taken. Believe me. I've been called worse."

He closed the suitcase. "You're quite a woman, Miss Stein." He took the suitcase from the table.

"Thank you, Mr. Dixon. Good-bye, now."

That night, Frank lit a small wood fire in the stove in one corner of his flat and settled into his bed with two short stories he had taken from the suitcase, which lay now atop his small, square dining table. He looked forward to returning the bag and its contents to Mrs. Hemingway in the morning. He knew her smile would be wide and warm. Also, it would be interesting to meet her husband, he thought, who seemed to inspire such deep passions from women as different as Hadley Hemingway and Gertrude Stein. The pages in Frank's hands were thin and fragile, as if they had yellowed and aged in some extraordinary way during their disappearance. He looked at the words. This Hemingway was not a very good typist, he thought. No matter. Perhaps Hemingway's stories were worth reading, whatever Miss Stein's appraisal. The first, which was titled "The Trouble with People," began like this: "That summer Nick and Harvey Greer were on good terms with a girl named Marie-Georges who worked in a café where they used to go on the Ile Saint Louis. . . ."

Frank fell asleep before finishing the story—not because he was bored or disliked Mr. Hemingway's work, but because he liked it very much; that is, he perceived in its rhythms something worthwhile, which filled him with such satisfaction at having recovered the suitcase that he allowed his body to relax and settle into the linen of his bedsheets.

The next morning he started for the Hemingway residence at 74 Rue du Cardinal Lemoine. Mrs. Hemingway had told him that she and her husband lived above a sawmill. Frank thought he knew the place. Not far. It was gray outside; weighty clouds hovered in the west, promising rain by midmorning, but Frank's spirits remained sunny. In the street, the scent of coffee was lovely. Frank looked at his wristwatch; it was too early to call on the Hemingways. He stopped at the Select for a café au lait, settling at a table on the sidewalk. He set the suitcase at his feet and glanced up and down the Boulevard du Montparnasse. He watched the stop-and-go traffic sign flip from one imperative to the next and back again. Stop-go, stop-go, all day, all night. Rattling horse cabs clippety-clopped past the café; stinking taxi traffic weaved, horns honking, among the carriages; pedestrians moved through the spaces that opened between the vehicles. Up the sidewalk, beneath a chestnut tree, a man sold windup, jumping-frog toys, which he had set on a blanket in neat rows. He called out in the morning air: "*Grenouilles, grenouilles!*" Frogs, frogs!

Frank settled back in his chair, lighting a Gauloise. He rarely allowed himself time for reflection—too dangerous.

But on this cloudy morning, he felt safe in his own head. He recalled his college job busing tables in New Jersey, undertaken not to pay for his tuition (which was covered by a generous aunt) but to pay for the flying lessons at Bell Field that occupied the better part of his attention during his final, less-than-distinguished sophomore year at Princeton. Frank loved flying—being in the sky made him feel less lonely for Joe. Sometimes, he even thought he caught glimpses of his brother's Nieuport 17 in the shadowed regions of the clouds—impossible, of course. These days, Frank's scant bank account permitted him to rent a Caudron only once or twice a year, which was just enough to keep his pilot's license current. He took a final drag on his cigarette, left money on the table, rose, and started down the Boulevard Raspail toward the Hemingways' home.

Passing the Luxembourg Gardens, he noticed geraniums in bloom.

He thought of his hometown girl, Callie Shaw, who three years before had broken off their relationship when he told her he was leaving college early to come to France. Now she was married to Tony Prito, Frank's old friend from Bayport. Had Callie been at Frank's side now, he thought, she'd have made him stop to breathe the scented air; she was always one for flowers. Sure, she had once promised to accompany him here. But who can truly make a promise? For example, on that last day at the docks in New York—where thousands of well-wishers called farewells—Joe had promised his family to return safely from France. If Joe's promises could not be trusted, whose could? Frank did not blame Callie for being absent now.

He stopped. Callie slipped from his thoughts.

The suitcase.

He had forgotten it back at the café.

The suitcase did not turn up the next day or the next.

Two weeks after its final disappearance, a note arrived at Frank's apartment; it was from Miss Stein, who had ascertained in that time that the suitcase had not been returned to Hemingway. She thanked Frank for his "decision," suggesting that it "reflected the most refined and far-seeing literary sensibility." He almost threw her note away, anxious by now to forget the whole incident, but decided at the last moment that one day it might be interesting to accept Miss Stein's open invitation to call again at 27 Rue de Fleurus, where the pictures on the walls were amazing and the brandy in the sideboard delicious. Besides, who knew? Perhaps he had done this Hemingway fellow a favor after all.

He turned and broke into a run, pushing past the same women he had smiled at moments before while strolling in the opposite direction. He felt his heart race and his blood pump in the cords of his neck. How could he be so stupid! he wondered, crossing the Rue d'Assas against the traffic sign. He pushed through a crowd of men in straw boaters and rounded the corner to the sidewalk outside the Café Select, praying no one had noticed the forgotten suitcase.

The suitcase was gone, stolen once more.

Frank wandered the Quarter the rest of the morning, hoping to catch a glimpse of the suitcase in the hands of a careless thief or the window of a just-opened pawnshop. No such glimpse. It began to rain. He did not bother to return home for his coat. He wandered the Quarter through the afternoon, glimpsing Hemingway himself drinking inside the Rotonde, which was crowded with those who had slippe inside to stay warm and dry. Hemingway was laughing, aware of what he had just lost again. What could he Hemingway's wife? Frank wondered. Nothing, he th He would return her money. He wandered the quar past dark, scuttling beneath the electric lights, soake eled, desperate—like one of the Conan Doyle ch had not believed were real.

At about midnight he returned home, exh

In his apartment, awful silence. The two tyr that Frank had fallen asleep reading th remained on the floor beside the bed. He h them back in the suitcase. Now he pic Trouble with People." "Out on the Wa author's name. Frank could not retu these two stories alone. He put the of his desk and locked them away, bottle of rum that he kept beside

Mid-Atlantic

In this moment, when it seemed that there was no hope of rescue, it was but natural that Nancy Drew's thoughts should turn to her father.

Carolyn Keene
The Bungalow Mystery

Carolyn Keene stood beside the polished wooden railing at midship on the main deck of the ocean liner *Mauretania.* Salt air whipped across her face. Below, the ship's massive hull sliced the cold, gray Atlantic, leaving a white scar on the water's surface that stretched from the ship's stern back toward New York as far as Carolyn could see. Although France remained a day away, this was the hour Carolyn had anticipated since the first night of the crossing, when she had made the acquaintance of Mr. F. Scott Fitzgerald in the first-class smoking room.

In the salon that first evening, Carolyn had accompanied Count Orlovsky, the eighty-two-year-old Russian who some months before had taken a liking to her chapbook, *11 poems* (self-published in an edition of 200), and had thereafter volunteered to sponsor Carolyn's Atlantic crossing and introductions to the literati in Paris. After the count had retired to his cabin, Fitzgerald told Carolyn that her confident manner as the only woman in a room full of cigar-wielding industrialists, titled barons, millionaire bankers, and moving-picture impresarios had suggested that she might be just the woman he had hoped to meet on this passage.

"You see, there's the matter of my wife," Fitzgerald said.

Carolyn had seen the famous Zelda boarding with Scott. Zelda was small, her face heart-shaped, and her hair a glistening gold. Their five-year-old daughter, Scottie, walked between them, her hands held on each side by her parents. Carolyn had thought they were a lovely family, though she noticed that Zelda's eyes did not meet anyone else's, even when the captain shook their hands at the top of the gang-plank.

"My wife is . . ." He stopped.

"Yes?"

Fitzgerald took a flask from his hip pocket. He offered it to Carolyn (who declined), then tossed back a drink. With the first gulp, color began to drain from his already fair skin; Carolyn had never seen anything like it—his face passed from vitality to a morbid pallor with a single swig. "You see, Zelda is fragile and sometimes I'm unable to watch over her myself. I mean, when I drink a lot." He waited, then nodded as if Carolyn had said something. "No, I don't drink just for alcohol's sake, you understand," he said. "That would be mere indulgence. I drink because I'm certain it's a fundamental source of my creativity, which I have a responsibility to nurture. I have a family to support, you understand. But, of course, sometimes . . ." He looked at Carolyn with blue eyes that were not as clear now as they had been a moment before.

"What is it you'd like me to do, Mr. Fitzgerald?" she asked.

"I'd like you to call me Scott."

"All right."

"I want you to watch over Zelda for the next few days. Just from time to time, because she doesn't always watch out for herself and I, well, as I was saying, I don't always watch over her because I . . ." He stopped.

"Because you drink?"

"Because I am a failure."

"Oh, no. My God, I would like to fail like you."

"No you wouldn't."

"I thought your last book was brilliant."

He smiled but did not meet her gaze.

"I wasn't going to say anything," she continued. "I thought you'd find it boring. You must hear such things all the time. But now I understand that it's wrong not to let you know how much I like your work."

"Will you help me with Zelda?"

"Are you asking me to spy on her?"

"No, no. I'm just asking you to watch out for her."

"Why? What are you afraid might happen?"

"Whenever we're on a ship, I fear she might . . . fall overboard."

"Over the rail?"

"Sure. She could slip, or whatever. I should be vigilant, but sometimes I'm not."

"Are you telling me you're afraid she'll jump?"

He looked away. "I love her."

"Then what makes you think she'd jump?"

"Last year in Antibes she threw herself down a flight of stairs."

"Why?"

"She had fallen in love with another man."

"Oh." Carolyn did not know how to answer, taken aback by Fitzgerald's candor. "That must have been very painful."

"Yes, for everyone involved, I'm sure," he answered.

"But with time."

"Oh, yes, with time," he said. "Zelda and I are doing all right. I'm just concerned that there be no accidents to interfere with what time can do for us. You understand, I'm sure. You seem such a sensible person, Carolyn." Then he smiled. "Sensible, even if you are mixed up in this crazy writing thing."

"I'll be happy to watch out for you and Zelda in whatever way I can."

"Thank you." He sat back in his chair.

"This 'writing thing'?" she asked. "Is it as crazy as all that?"

"Oh, yes, but that's what makes it worthwhile."

After leaving River Heights, Carolyn had spent six months with cousins in Chicago before embarking on a year-long European tour with her septuagenarian Aunt Sylvia. Afterwards, Carolyn had landed in New York City, where she planned to work in advertising or study American history at Columbia. Greenwich Village was not initially part of her plan. Artists, musicians, bootleg whiskey . . . Within a week, however, she had moved her luggage out of the Wellington and into a single room above the Proper Pagan Tea Room, where she began waiting tables. Naturally, Aunt Sylvia disapproved of both the broken-down, cold-water flat and the job. But that didn't matter to Carolyn. She was no longer engaged in a tour of the respectable European attractions found in her aunt's Michelin guidebook. In Greenwich Village, Carolyn discovered new kinds of art (not in museums, but in speakeasies like the Hell Hole on West

Fourth Street, where jazz wafted with the scent of beer onto the crowded sidewalks). She began writing poetry, for which more than one new friend suggested she had a gift.

Her father, however, disapproved.

"Your stepmother and I worry about what is becoming of you," he wrote.

"But you don't understand how hard I'm working to create something worthwhile," she replied in a letter home. "For example, my chapbook of eleven poems has been drawn from a selection of more than two hundred I've written these past months."

"Your stepmother and I worry about what has *become* of you," he replied. "We know about that Greenwich Village environment. We never dreamed you'd become dissolute."

What followed seemed innocent and inevitable to Carolyn: she learned that the best modernist poets were working in Paris—the wealthy Count Orlovsky liked her work—she booked passage. What could be objectionable about that?

"Your stepmother and I are losing hope for you," her father wrote when he learned of her move abroad.

What did they want from her? she wondered.

Now, nearing teatime on the next-to-last day of the Atlantic crossing, Carolyn took a small journal from the inside pocket of her coat, turning her back to the railing to protect the pages from the mist that floated up from the churned sea. Scott was due here almost any minute. She had told him she had an important question to ask. He had agreed to do his best to answer. To pass the time, she opened the book. Inside she had jotted the following notes:

Met Zelda at breakfast this morning after agreeing to help Scott last night. She spoke eloquently to the entire table about dancing as self-expression, both the kind of dancing practiced on board the ship with graceful partners (excluding Scott, it seems) and also in the ballet classes she intends to join in Paris. Zelda = world's oldest beginning ballerina? But Heaven help whoever points out that the time to take up ballet is in one's childhood.

Nonetheless, Scott encourages her and seems to believe she can make up for lost years. Who knows? She has a quick, brutal wit. I like her. But I wouldn't want to be her. She washed down breakfast with a shot of gin. As we were leaving breakfast, she asked me what I saw in Orlovsky besides his money. I explained that there was nothing between us except money—my poetry, his patronage. She laughed and replied that the only reasonable arrangement between any man and woman was one of money tendered for services rendered. Of course, she was just joking, but Scott seemed unhappy with her sentiment. I don't think she means half of what she says. I wonder if Scott can always tell which half is which?

Before dinner I met Zelda and little Scottie on deck. Scott was in their stateroom. With a tiny brush, Zelda painted outfits for her homemade paper dolls, which are closely modeled on Scott, Scottie, and Zelda herself. When each tiny costume was finished, Zelda placed it atop a cutout figure. Scottie laughed with joy, though Zelda did not allow her to touch the paper dolls for fear she'd tear them. A gust raced along the deck, and Zelda pressed the paper dolls into the table to keep them from blowing away. In that moment, I imagined the Zelda doll floating over the railing, away from the other two dolls, and down into the sea, after which Scott (the real one and not the paper doll) would hurl himself over the rail to save the cardboard image. . . .

Carolyn returned the journal to her coat pocket. It had been three days since she had made this last entry; in the meantime, she had been either too drunk or too hungover to write anything more. The Fitzgeralds drank like no one Carolyn had ever known, although these past two years she had kept company in Greenwich Village with more than a few tipplers. Sometimes, Scott's drunkenness seemed disproportionate to the amount of alcohol he consumed, Carolyn thought. He had a constitution like a child. At the same time, Zelda possessed a disquieting ability to seem more sober than she actually was. Between the revelries, however, the Fitzgeralds had been kind to Carolyn. Scott had spoken to her like a colleague, Zelda like a friend. Even Orlovsky seemed pleased—and why not? Here was his protégée socializing with the most famous literary couple in America. But it was neither literature nor fame that most fascinated Carolyn about the Fitzgeralds. It was that they had hurt one another for so long and yet still seemed to share a love—or something like it. With only one full day left onboard the *Mauretania,* Carolyn decided to understand how the two managed it.

"I worry for you, my dear," Orlovsky had said that morning when Carolyn told him what she hoped to learn. She and the count were taking breakfast at a linen-covered table on the observation deck (the only place Carolyn could speak loudly enough for the old man to hear without alerting every other diner to each word spoken). "Do the Fitzgeralds know you're studying them?"

Carolyn reached across the table to help the old man crack his boiled egg. "They know I observe," she answered. "In fact, Scott asked me to do so. On the first night of the crossing."

"They're nice enough people, my dear," he said, wrapping his blanket about his frail shoulders though the sky was clear and the day warm. "But remember, if the Fitzgeralds are role models for anything, it's dissipation."

"Yes, but at least they'll have dissipated *together*," Carolyn answered.

"Drink your tea," he instructed.

A few hours later, at a private lunch, Zelda listened patiently to Carolyn's questions about love before answering that she had nothing whatsoever to impart on the subject. "I've never understood it," she said. "I never will. Because I never want to understand it."

"Then how can you ever trust it?" Carolyn asked.

"Who says love should be trustworthy? It's love, for God's sake. Not a puppy."

"But if you understood it . . ."

Zelda stopped her. "If you understood it you'd go mad."

"I think not understanding it makes a person mad."

"Dear Carolyn." Zelda took a long drink. "Do you know the Greek myths in which mortals seek to know things meant only for the gods?"

Carolyn nodded.

"Irony, irony, irony," Zelda said, her Alabama accent turning the words to music. "Always irony in those myths. That's what makes them true. Do you want to know what I think?"

"That's why I asked," Carolyn said.

"I believe you could understand love," she explained, "but in doing so you'd immediately lose all other rational faculties—your brain would go dark, like when an electrical circuit blows in a house. Overload. Darkness! Of course, I can only speak for myself. Understand, whatever I have that passes for a rational mind now in my weary, overcrowded head exists only because I've always protected it from the contagion of love's contemplation. Understand, my dear?"

"I think so."

"Thinking and feeling are two separate spheres," Zelda concluded. "Don't think about feeling, Carolyn. And never waste your feeling on thoughts. And one last thing . . ."

"What?"

"Don't ever say another word about any of this sticky shit to me, please."

"Okay," Carolyn answered.

"I mean it," Zelda finished. "Say the word 'love' again and I'll throw myself into the sea."

"Sorry."

"Will you have another glass of wine with lunch, Carolyn?"

In truth, it had been Scott's views on the subject that most interested Carolyn. It was Scott who had been betrayed the year before. From another deck, Carolyn heard a jazz band. Perhaps Scott was there, listening to the music. Drinking. Perhaps he was already drunk. He might never show, Carolyn thought. She watched the horizon, razor sharp in every direction. Blue above, blue below, but never the same shade of blue anywhere she looked—from here to America, from here to France, from ocean to sky. She removed her journal once more, along with the stub of a pencil, and wrote on one page:

blue is
always blue
in its own
way

She looked at the little poem for a long time.

Then she tore the page from the book, wadded it into a ball, and tossed it into the Atlantic, far below.

"Carolyn?"

She turned.

Scott stood five feet away. "What are you doing?" he asked.

"Nothing."

"Are you making wishes?" he asked. "My grandmother used to write wishes on slips of paper, toss them into the sea, and wait for the gods of the deep to make them come true."

"Did they come true?"

"Sometimes."

Carolyn was happy to see that he was sober.

"What are you wishing for, Carolyn?"

"Just now, I guess I was wishing I was a real poet."

"You are a poet, Carolyn."

"You've looked at my poems?"

He nodded. "Good stuff."

Suddenly, she needed him to be honest. She caught his eyes with hers. "I said a real poet, Scott."

"Oh, 'real.' You mean, as in very, very good?"

"Yes."

He nodded. "That's a good wish."

"Do you think it can ever come true for me?" she asked.

"Sure."

"Don't just say that. Please, tell me the truth."

He looked out at the sea. "Is this what you wanted to talk to me about?"

"No, but now that we're at it . . ." She waited.

"Life is long and unpredictable, Carolyn. Especially when it comes to art. I mean, who can say?"

"You can say," she answered. "That's why I'm asking, Scott. Will it ever come true for me?"

"I can't say."

"You can. Please tell me the truth."

"No."

"No, you can't say?" she asked. "Or no, it won't happen?"

"No, Carolyn. The poetry won't work for you. Not in the way you want. Not ever."

She looked away.

"I'm sorry, Carolyn. I could be wrong."

"You're not wrong."

In that moment, Carolyn realized that writing poetry had never been first in her heart or mind, whatever her declarations. For her, poetry had been a diversion, a means of connecting with others, a rich therapy, but nothing more. Scott was right: she was not a "real" poet—otherwise, wouldn't she want to throw herself into the sea just now instead of feeling liberated, like a schoolgirl relieved of a homework assignment? Orlovsky and her friends were wrong about her work, she thought, as were her suitors in the Village, who more than once had commented (sometimes to their romantic advantage) that her poetry displayed an "intoxicating sensuality."

"Actually, I asked you here to talk about love," she said to Scott.

"Oh, a subject I'm even less qualified to talk about."

"I wanted to ask you how to forgive."

"Forgive what?"

"Betrayal."

"A lover?"

She shook her head. "Oh, there've been a few scoundrels. Aren't there always? But I'm not thinking of any of them now."

"Then who?"

"My father."

Scott said nothing.

"He and his wife don't approve of me," Carolyn said.

"Well, that's not so uncommon among parents."

"When I booked passage to Paris, I phoned him because I wanted to visit home before leaving," she continued. "It's been years. But he thought it best that I visit another time. 'When?' I asked. He had no answer. I was dumbfounded. I mean, who knows when I'll be back in the States? He and his wife have a two-year-old daughter I've never met. Her name's Rose. She's my half sister."

"That's very hard," Scott said.

"These past years my life in the Village has not been consistent with River Heights sensibilities, I guess. At least not with her sensibilities."

"Whose? Your stepmother's?"

Carolyn nodded.

"But what of your father?" Scott asked. "Why does he allow this to happen?"

"That's the part I don't understand."

"You may just have to let it all go," he suggested.

"My new life?"

"No, River Heights."

"Sure, but how?"

"Look, 'letting go' is not exactly my forte."

"But you've managed to forgive."

He shrugged.

"What does one do?" she pressed.

"I can tell you what not to do."

"Yes?"

"Don't start drinking," he said. "It isn't enough by itself, no matter how faithfully you devote yourself to the pursuit."

"But you've forgiven Zelda."

"Have I?"

"Well, you love her still. That's clear. And you can't love her if you haven't come to terms with what's happened between the two of you. Isn't that right?"

"'Come to terms with' and 'forgive' may not be the same thing."

"No?"

"Christ, Carolyn. If I knew the answers to all these questions, do you think my own life would be the way it is?"

"Your life is beautiful."

He said nothing.

"Most people would like to be you," she continued.

"I'm sorry, but have you observed nothing at all aboard this ship?" Then he turned and walked away.

She watched him go.

That night at dinner Carolyn told Count Orlovsky that she would no longer avail herself of his patronage because she was finished writing poetry.

"But why stop, my dear?" Orlovsky asked.

"Oh, I've never really been comfortable reaching for metaphors and similes."

"What poet is?"

"Yes, but some poets find words that are worth the discomfort. Whereas I . . ." She looked away.

"You're young, Carolyn. Your best work is ahead of you."

She shook her head. "My sensibilities are inconsistent with true modernist writing."

"Why is that?"

"I'm not altogether a modern, I guess."

He said nothing.

Carolyn shrugged. "A girl can't help being who she is."

The old man smiled. "Ah, Carolyn, why would you want to be any different than you are?"

"Why?" She laughed. "Let me count the ways . . ."

Orlovsky stopped her. "Look, my dear, you may think you're finished with writing, but that doesn't necessarily mean writing is finished with you."

After dinner, Carolyn knocked at the Fitzgeralds' stateroom door. She wanted to explain to them that she understood now that they were not exotic half-angels but mere human beings and that being human was quite enough to ask of anyone.

A woman in a nanny's outfit answered the door. "The Fitzgeralds are out," she said.

From inside the stateroom little Scottie cried out, "Hi, Miss Carolyn!"

"Hi, Scottie."

"Would you like to come in for a moment to say goodnight?" the nanny asked.

"Yes."

"I was just putting Scottie to bed."

"Will you read me a story?" Scottie asked Carolyn.

The nanny grinned her approval.

"Okay," Carolyn answered.

Scottie lay bundled on a small sofa beneath two portholes. The sofa had been laid with bed linens and pillows and was just long enough for Scottie's five-year-old body, which was scrubbed clean and pink and dressed now in a white nightgown. She held a baby doll. The door to the

Fitzgeralds' bedroom was closed. The stateroom smelled of orchids, though Carolyn saw no fresh flowers.

"I have some books over there," Scottie said, pointing to the coffee table.

Carolyn picked up the books. She pulled a chair from the desk over to the sofa and sat beside the girl. Scottie was as lovely as her parents, and she was fresh in ways Carolyn could not imagine either Scott or Zelda ever having been, though she knew there must once have been such a time for each.

"Which book would you like me to read?" Carolyn asked.

"Doesn't matter," Scottie answered, pulling the covers up to her chin. "They're all the same."

"What do you mean?"

"Princesses rescued by princes," Scottie explained. "Doesn't matter which you pick, Miss Carolyn. My mother is a princess, you know. Which means that I am too, even though nobody knows it, because I haven't been raised in the gracious manner of the South, like my mother."

"What if instead of reading you a story I just make one up for you?"

"Okay," Scottie said, cuddling her doll.

"All right. Well. Let's see." How to begin?

"Does the story begin, 'Once upon a time'?" Scottie suggested.

"Sure. Like this: Once upon a time there lived a fine girl who was as brave as any prince or knight. One day the girl . . ."

"Does the girl have a name?" Scottie interrupted. She was naturally quite savvy about storytelling.

"Oh, a name. Well, sure. Let's see, what's your doll's name?"

"Nancy," she answered.

"That's quite a coincidence," Carolyn said. "Nancy just happens to be our heroine's name too."

"Yeah?"

Carolyn nodded. "And Nancy is a fine girl. She drives a blue roadster and . . ."

"What's her last name?" Scottie interrupted.

"Oh. Well, let's see. It's not Keene, like mine. Or Fitzgerald, like yours."

"No, of course not."

"It's Smith!" Carolyn said.

"Smith?" Scottie made a face.

The child's standards for bedtime stories were understandably high.

"Jones?" Carolyn suggested.

"That's worse."

"Oh, right." Suddenly, Carolyn's mind was blank. "Tell me, Scottie, what's your favorite thing to do?"

"For fun?"

Carolyn nodded.

"I like to draw."

"That's it!" Carolyn said. "Her last name is Draw."

"Nancy Draw?"

"No, Drew. How's that?"

"Oh, that's good."

Carolyn's confidence returned. "Yes, and Nancy lives in a town in the Middle West of America with her father who loves her very much. Nancy is a poet. No, not a poet. Better. Wait till you hear!"

"What?" Scottie asked.

"Nancy is a girl detective."

"Oh, perfect!" Scottie said as the story commenced.

Clues on the Riviera

(three years later)

A speeding shadow in the sky resolved itself into the shape of an airplane, which began to descend in wide spirals.

Franklin W. Dixon
The Great Airport Mystery

Sorely perplexed and a trifle discouraged, Nancy Drew admitted to herself that the mystery was likely to prove even more baffling than she had anticipated.

Carolyn Keene
The Mystery at Lilac Inn

The first time Frank Dixon ever saw Carolyn Keene was from the air at almost 160 kilometers per hour. At such a speed she was little more than a blur two hundred feet below. Nonetheless, he noticed her, because on other mornings Gerald Murphy, the American bon vivant who played host to many famous artists and writers here in the south of France, raked the rocks from the beach outside his villa alone. This morning Gerald had a partner. Frank knew the young woman raking the sand with him was not Gerald's wife, Sara, because Mrs. Murphy was just then in the passenger seat of the Breguet 14 directly in front of Frank, soaring over the glimmering Mediterranean and waving down to her husband on the beach.

Gerald waved up to her.

Frank looked back over his shoulder as he banked up and out toward the sea. The woman below did not wave, but shielded her eyes with her hand to see the biplane against the glare of morning.

Sara turned back toward Frank, her face flushed, her pearls sparkling in the sunlight. "Lovely, lovely!" she shouted above the roar of the engine and the rush of air. Frank nodded and gave her the thumbs-up sign. He knew Sara referred to the view. High above the Mediterranean one could see along the Riviera as far east as Monte Carlo, as far west as Cannes and Saint-Tropez. Yes, lovely. But Frank thought Sara might just as well have been referring to the woman on the beach, whose posture and attitude intrigued him: one hand shielding her eyes, the other balancing her weight against the rake. It was as if she were more interested in what she saw than how she was seen—a rare attitude among these glamorous and brilliant people, who lived their lives as if they were being constantly observed by posterity. Well, he would give her something to watch, he thought. He pushed the stick forward and dropped the plane into a dive, racing away from the shore. In the front seat, Sara Murphy threw her hands into the air above her head and let out a scream like a girl on a roller coaster.

"Lovely, lovely," she shouted.

Frank leveled the aircraft sixty feet above the Mediterranean; he pushed the throttle to 170 kilometers per hour and set his eyes on the blue horizon.

"Oh, Frank, this is the life!" Sara cried, turning back once more.

"Do you want to loop-the-loop?" he yelled.

Her smile disappeared. "No!"

Frank had met the Murphys three days before, having arrived in Cap d'Antibes with a letter of introduction from his friend, Gertrude Stein, who visited the Murphys' Villa America whenever she and Alice traveled to the Riviera. Now, Gertrude remained behind at 27 Rue de Fleurus with a head cold. In her letter to Gerald and Sara she had described Frank Dixon as "a good friend and an even better aviator." Gertrude had never seen Frank fly but by now had come to trust in his professional competence (if only she knew what had really become of Hemingway's lost suitcase! he often thought). A few weeks before, Gertrude had heard through her on-again-off-again friend Picasso that Gerald Murphy was looking for a pilot to take houseguests flying on occasional weekends. He had acquired a Breguet 14 that had recently belonged to a neighbor, a pilot who awoke one morning suddenly afraid of heights. "Yes, Frank," Gertrude had said in the dining room over shared glasses of the pure fruit *alcools* that Alice distilled. "I believe this would be a productive experience for you. I'll write a letter. You need a vacation. Paris will not crumble without your private investigating for a little while."

"I'm in the middle of a number of cases."

"Nonsense," Gertrude answered. "Adulterers, runaways, embezzlers . . . what's the hurry?"

"That's not the problem," he answered. Flying had lost much of its appeal for Frank. Once, being in the sky made him feel closer to Joe. These days, however, flying only reminded Frank of what he had failed to accomplish these last few years—no sign of Lt. Joe Dixon in the whole damn country. "I'd like to fly their plane, Gertrude, but I don't know . . ."

"I already understand that there's plenty you don't know, young man," she interrupted. "But what you don't know doesn't matter to me. It's what I know that matters. And it's what should matter to you too. Besides, I'm never wrong when it comes to my friends."

"It's not as simple as it seems."

"I understand," she said. "Remember, I know you're not as simple as you seem."

"Hmm, is that a compliment?"

In the beginning, Frank wondered why Gertrude took such a friendly interest in him. All of her other young friends were writers or painters or composers. They courted her approval and offered with the timidity of schoolchildren their latest work for her criticism. Frank thought the title of her latest book, *The Making of Americans,* was appropriate. It seemed to him that so many hopeful American artists wanted Gertrude to do just that—to *make* them, as if she might with her peasant hands mold their sensibilities as well as their careers and reputations. Frank did not have a painting to show her or musical composition to play for her (and he surely wasn't going to show her his gathering number of novice short stories, all well begun, all abandoned incomplete). He hadn't even the patience to get through reading all nine-hundred-and-something pages of *The Making of Americans.* At last it occurred to him that Gertrude might be interested in him *because* he was not using her to further an artistic career. When he proposed as much she nodded vigorously.

"Yes, dear boy. You're not an artist. But you're an actual character."

"Me? No." Frank shook his head. "I've met your friends, Gertrude. They're characters. All plumed serpents. Every one of them. Not me. Please, I'm just an old brown shoe."

"Yes," she said. "They are indeed plumed serpents. But here is the difference: their characters, however exotic or intriguing, have been crafted self-consciously from their own gifted imaginations. Nothing unusual about that. Not for an artist. Anyone half-talented can make himself the leading character in whatever drama or comedy he creates for himself. Look at Hemingway. He is his own best creation. Always will be. Everyone knows that. That's just the way it is."

"And me?"

"Well, you may not be as brilliant as they are, that's true."

"Thanks."

"You're no plumed serpent, my boy."

"Then why . . ."

She stopped him. "Why? Because you are a character in a drama of which you are not the author. Do you understand?"

"No."

"Exactly!" she said.

"You've lost me, Gertrude."

"Good. Now I want to lose you physically as well as intellectually. For the time being, at least. All right? Go to Cap d'Antibes, my dear boy. Fly the Murphys' plane. Muss your hair. Get out of my house." She stood.

"Right now?"

"Yes." She handed him the letter of reference. "You'll like the Murphys. It's impossible not to, despite their money. Now go, I have work to do."

He put the letter in his pocket and left 27 Rue de Fleurus without a word.

Sometimes Gertrude's behavior was demeaning, intrusive. Nevertheless, she was most often right.

In the morning he boarded the train for Cap d'Antibes.

Now, he banked the Breguet 14 back toward the shore and the Murphys' Villa America.

"What a wonderful ride!" Sara called.

Approaching the shore, Frank noticed that Gerald Murphy was raking the sand alone. Frank wondered if the woman he had seen beside Gerald had been real, or if she had been another of the occasional hallucinations Frank experienced when flying. He landed in a pasture behind the villa. Other guests of the Murphys made their way to the plane to partake of the recreational flying that occupied Frank until well into the afternoon. Of course, he could not know that the mysterious woman was simply afraid of heights. When he left the grounds at the end of the day, walking back to the hotel room the Murphys had secured for him in the old town, he thought it just as likely that he had imagined her from a mere glint of sunlight at the edge of his goggles. True, he might have asked any of the guests about her, but he had long before learned that there is little a passenger appreciates less than an aviator whose vision seems inconsistent with his or her own.

Later that day, Carolyn Keene sat alone at a table upon which were an arrangement of violets, a bottle of Cinzano, and two empty water tumblers. It was lovely on the thirty-foot-wide terrace of the Villa America—the Mediterranean shimmered below. Most of the other guests napped in their rooms inside the house. Siesta time. Carolyn glanced at her wristwatch. Two-twenty. Hemingway was late. Had he forgotten their meeting? It wasn't like Pauline to let him do so, she thought. Carolyn considered going to the main house to look for him but decided that would seem too aggressive. Or too needy, which for Hemingway was much worse. Next, she considered returning to her own room to leave an empty, and thereby dignified, place here at the table when he arrived. But she did not want to sit alone in her room merely to assuage her pride. Still, she couldn't have Hemingway find her merely waiting for his arrival. She wished she had brought a book to read—anything but his new one, *The Sun*

Also Rises, which she liked but did not want to seem to fawn over. Hemingway was already too full of himself, she thought. He had been something of a local hero even before his novel's publication. A handful of published stories, the weight of his personality, and his renowned "potential" had of their own been sufficient to make him a favorite of the literary crowd in the Quarter and the gossip columnists of the *Paris Herald.* They made frequent mention of his split with his first wife, Hadley, and subsequent marriage to Pauline Pfeiffer, Carolyn's editor at the Paris office of the fashion magazine *Vogue.*

The air smelled of nearby fields of lavender.

From beside her chair, Carolyn lifted a large, brightly colored cotton handbag, which she had bought that morning at a flea market in Nice. She removed a cigarette lighter and a pack of Gauloises. Replacing the lighter, she noticed her new manuscript stuffed inside the handbag. Yes, here was something to do. She removed the eight typed pages from the bag, setting them face up on the table beside the violets. She reached behind her ear for a pencil—a habit she had acquired working this past year in the magazine's office— but found no pencil. Once more, she took up her handbag to sort through it. Still, no pencil. She dropped the bag to the dusty ground and glanced at the first page of the manuscript:

> The Simple Black Dress, or How Coco Triumphed
> by Carolyn Keene

Drivel, she thought. Still, she had worked hard on the piece, which was to be her first cover article for the magazine. It was not the sort of writing that mattered most to Carolyn. She picked up the eight pages. They were as light as a cloud. Almost as insubstantial too. However, if Hemingway were to find Carolyn line-editing the pages of her article, he might be more inclined to take seriously her questions about writing a novel of her own. But what kind of writer travels without a pencil? She poured herself a drink of Cinzano.

Ah, yes, drinking.

Hemingway was bound to recognize drinking as a "writerly" activity, she thought. She looked around. No one within sight. She took the bottle of Cinzano, leaned half out of her chair, and poured three or four tall glassfuls into the soft dirt of a well-tended flower box at the edge of the terrace. Hemingway would infer that the bottle had been full at two o'clock. And now, a mere twenty minutes later . . . half gone! Lady Brett–type drinking. Yes, she thought, who needs a pencil as evidence of literary seriousness when one can display instead a half-empty bottle of alcohol and a still-sober disposition? If she played it right, Hemingway might challenge her to a boxing match or some such thing.

She set the half-empty bottle back on the table—then laughed aloud at her own foolishness. What did it matter what Hemingway thought?

"It matters not a damn," she said to herself.

But she knew that was a lie.

To Carolyn Keene what others thought always mattered. She wished it were different. Nonetheless, she remained her father's daughter. Despite her best efforts. Six thousand miles and a half-dozen lovers since she'd left River Heights, and still she had found no true way to stop being Carson Keene's "good little girl." Paris was crowded with dissolute American role models—Zelda Fitzgerald, Dorothy Parker, Caresse Crosby, the I-don't-care girls. Yet here Carolyn sat, attempting to seem more dissolute than she really was. She crossed her legs, then uncrossed them, then crossed them once more. She realized that she did not even know what a "natural" posture was. How to sit! Had she ever known "natural"? Even as a girl? Whatever's comfortable, she reminded herself. But that was the problem. She did not know what comfortable meant to her. She knew only what would appear comfortable and relaxed to others—so they in turn could actually feel comfortable and relaxed. Sometimes Carolyn felt very tired. Yet she never allowed herself to stop moving and thinking and doing because she dreaded what might overtake her if ever she did, which was this: an abiding terror that she was merely ridiculous and nothing more.

She sipped the Cinzano.

She hated the taste of alcohol.

"Oh, hell," she whispered.

She sipped more.

Then Hemingway appeared from around the corner of the house. He smiled and held his palms open at his sides in supplication. "I'm sorry to be late," he said. He had gained weight in the months he had been married to Pauline. A good sign for them, Carolyn thought. Hemingway, the happy husband. He'd probably take the weight off in the gym. Everything changes. "I was helping Gerald stock his boat, and I lost track of the hour," he continued. "So sorry."

"You're late?" Carolyn asked. She listened to her words, as if they had emerged of their own volition from her mouth. "Hadn't we planned to meet at two-thirty? Aren't you a little early?"

"Oh?"

"Yes, I'm sure."

"Really?"

She motioned for him to sit. "I just got here myself. You know, to enjoy the view for a few minutes. Get a little peace and quiet. But sit down, please. I'm glad it's worked out like this. I'd hate to have left you waiting in the confusion."

"Two-thirty?" he asked, sitting down. He poured himself a drink from the half-empty bottle.

She swallowed what remained in her own glass.

"Coulda sworn it was two."

"Damn it, Hem. If it had been two o'clock, do you think I'd still be waiting for you?"

He laughed. "That a girl," he said.

"Is Scott tight yet?" she asked.

He nodded.

"And what's Pauline doing?"

"Napping," he said. "She's a hell of a girl, isn't she, Carolyn?"

Carolyn nodded. "She's been such a help with the Chanel piece."

"She likes your work."

"I'm glad to hear it." Then she sat back in her chair. Silent. As if it had been Hemingway who had asked to meet.

"So, what can I do for you, Carolyn?"

"I wanted to talk to you."

"About?"

"I'm writing a novel."

"Very good."

"I'm about a hundred and twenty pages into it."

"The main thing is just to keep going," he said. He drank the Cinzano. "It's a fight, I know. Writing's a bastard, Carolyn. But you gotta kick its ass or it'll kick yours, believe me."

"I'm learning that."

"It's you versus the blank page."

"I wanted to run a sentence past you."

"A sentence?"

She nodded.

"Okay."

"The book's about a girl detective," she explained.

"Detective. That's good. Is she 'hardboiled'?"

"She's only sixteen years old. How 'hardboiled' can she be?"

"Well, that depends. Some of those Indian girls I met up in Michigan . . ." He stopped.

She waited.

There was no more to Hemingway's story. "How's this sentence of yours go?" he asked.

"Like this." Carolyn spoke from memory: "'Nancy, a bright girl of sixteen, leaned over the library table to address her father, who sat reading a newspaper by the study lamp.'"

Hemingway nodded.

"That's it," she said.

"Okay. Fine."

"It's where I've left off in the novel."

"All right."

"Well, what do you think?"

"Of the sentence, as a sentence?"

She nodded. "You're quite famous for your sentences."

"It's fine."

She considered. "Fine as in refined to high level of competence?" she asked. "Or fine as in merely passable or sufficient?"

"Maybe we should talk about the plot of your novel instead of just one sentence," he suggested.

"The whole plot? Oh, I don't want to burden you, Ernest. Isn't a whole plot quite a lot to tackle at one sitting?"

"No, but one sentence is quite a lot."

"Oh?"

"Sentences are serious business, my dear girl."

"Of course."

He drank and turned toward the sea. "Too serious, perhaps, for a location as picturesque as this. Plots, you understand, lend themselves far better to recreation."

"Well, all right, but . . ." She stopped.

He turned back to her. "So, tell me about your detective story."

"There's something you have to understand, Ernest."

"Yes?"

"I'm not just passing my time writing this book," she said. "It's not just a hobby, like needlepoint. I mean, it's not great literature, that's for sure. But I wouldn't have asked for your opinion of my sentence if I were just playing around."

"Oh, of course not."

"I don't intend to be one of those Quarterites who talk and talk and talk about writing a novel and then never do it."

"No, I never imagined that of you."

"So tell me."

"Tell you what?"

"Is something wrong with the sentence?"

He shrugged. "Not so much."

"Well, what?"

"What's the sentence again?"

"'Nancy, a bright girl of sixteen, leaned over the library table to address her father, who sat reading a newspaper by the study lamp,'" Carolyn said.

He nodded.

"Well?"

"Is her father a postcard?" Hemingway asked.

"What?"

"Well, she 'addresses' him."

"Oh," Carolyn nodded. "You know what I mean."

"Yes, but the word 'address.' It's a little formal, don't you think?"

"Their relationship is a bit on the formal side, I suppose," she answered. "Warm, but formal."

"And that's what you wanted to call attention to in this sentence?"

"Not really."

"But you have."

"I see. So I could have just written that she leaned over the table to 'speak' to him?"

"Unless you actually meant 'address.' Which entails some sort of formal delivery. As in Gettysburg."

"Okay."

"And speaking of that table," he continued. "A library table located in a study . . . Is there such a thing as a 'library table'? Do you mean the kind of table with dividers built onto its top for the purpose of providing private study space?"

"No, just a table."

"Then why not call it a table?"

"I see."

"And you describe the girl as being 'bright.'"

She nodded. "You're going to ask me now if she glows like radium, right?"

"Well, radium hadn't come to mind, but . . ."

"I was referring, of course, to her intelligence."

"And what does that look like?"

"You know what I mean," she answered.

"Yes, but as a reader, if I have to rely on what I already know, then why should I read your book?"

She nodded, glancing away.

"And what newspaper is her father reading?"

"You mean the *Chicago Tribune* or the *New York Times* or whichever?"

"And what section of the paper?"

"Does it make a difference?" she asked.

"All the difference."

"Oh."

She waited. He said nothing more.

"Is that it?" she asked.

He nodded.

"Well, that's quite a lot for just one sentence. Thank you, Ernest."

"It's hard to write a good sentence," he said. "But that's what makes it worth doing."

"Sure," she said.

"That a girl."

"Ernest?"

"Yes?"

"When you told me the sentence was 'fine,' were you just patronizing me?"

He picked up his empty glass. "I'm sorry," Hemingway answered. "I understand now how inappropriate that was. But so few people ever want the truth."

"Okay."

He held his hand across the table to shake. "Friends?"

She took his hand. "Sure."

"Good."

"To tell you the truth," she said, "I'm not so sure I don't prefer being patronized."

He shook his head. "You don't prefer it."

"You're right. I hate it."

"By the way, the sentence is not all bad, you know."

"Didn't you hear what I just said?"

"I'm not patronizing you."

"Oh?"

"It has a rhythm," he said. "And rhythm can't be taught, Carolyn. Syntax and detail can be practiced. Everybody can use a mentor at one time or another. But an instinct for language can't be taught."

"It's just a sentence."

"If you've taken the time to write it down, Carolyn, it's not just a sentence. It's the moon and stars."

She laughed. "Isn't that a bit dramatic, Ernest?"

"Not to me."

"Or me either," she admitted.

"Christ, you wouldn't want to get it perfect your first time out of the gate, would you, Carolyn?"

"Sure I would."

"Naturally, a good deal depends on what the girl has to say to her father," Hemingway continued.

"Oh, sure." She said nothing more.

"Well, what does she say to him?" Hemingway asked, refilling Carolyn's glass.

"I don't know what she says next. That's another thing I wanted to ask you about."

"I can't tell you what she says."

"I understand that. But I wanted to ask you if you thought it was advisable for a writer not to know all that happens in a story before she actually sits down and begins writing it. I mean, how does it work for you?"

"Is it all right?" Hemingway slapped his palm on the table. "Damn it, Carolyn, it's essential that you not know." The almost-empty bottle tipped. "That's what writing is for. To find out what your character says and all the things that happen as a result."

"Yeah?" She stood the bottle up once more.

"If you know everything before you start, there's no point in starting. Right? The money sure as hell doesn't justify anybody's work. Except some of those hacks in New York.

But I'd be no better than a pimp or a common thief if I ever wrote for money alone. Everybody in the Quarter knows that's how I feel."

"Of course."

"Damn right."

"So you write to find out what you think?"

"It's the only way ever to find out."

"What about people who aren't writers?"

"They never know."

"Never?"

"Poor bastards. They can only ever think they know."

"And there's a difference between 'thinking' you know and 'knowing'?"

"Yes."

"But how can you feel confident, when you begin writing a story, that when you finish it you'll have come up with anything worthwhile at all?" she asked.

"Don't worry about that," he said. "Just worry about the words, kid."

She had never been called "kid" by a man only a few years older than herself. Somehow, she didn't mind. "So I actually have to write down the words to find out what I already know?"

He nodded. "Crazy, isn't it?"

"Yeah," she said.

He glanced over to the Mediterranean. "Damn blue," he said.

She nodded. "Blue is always blue in its own way."

"Hmm," he said. "That's not a bad sentence. 'Blue in its own way . . .'"

"You don't think it's too much like Tolstoy?"

He laughed. "You mean unhappy families always being unhappy in their own ways?"

She nodded.

"I wouldn't worry about that, Carolyn."

"Okay."

"Besides, what do you know about unhappy families? Pauline tells me your upbringing was near idyllic."

"Oh, I don't know about that."

"Sure you do, Carolyn. It's the only thing any of us really knows a damn about. Our upbringings."

"Well then, my upbringing was not idyllic."

"No? Then what was it, Carolyn?"

She considered. "Ridiculous," she said.

In the late afternoon, Frank Dixon walked the cobbled road that led from the Villa America down to Antibes. After spending the past years in the bustle of Paris, the quiet was a good change. But quiet too can contain distractions, which for Frank arose as small voices discernible in his head only when no murmuring crowds, jazz music, or cab horns drowned them out. Frank had heard the voices before, in the quiet that settled over Paris for two or three hours before sunrise. Sometimes he feared them, though he understood that however distinct they might seem, they were always variations of his own voice—even when they assumed the tenor of his father's or mother's or brother's. Yes, his mother would love the lilacs here in Provence. Yes, his father would delight in the food. Yes, his brother would leap like a merman through the gentle swells of the bathtub-warm Mediterranean. Yes, the whole Dixon family would delight in the Côte d'Azur. But Joe was not here, Frank reminded himself, negotiating the cobbled road that led to the town square. No Father, no Mother, no Joe.

He looked about him as he walked.

Above the old town, a whitewashed fifteenth-century

fort guarded the citizens from invaders who no longer existed—or was it only defense by fort that no longer existed, while the next wave of invaders was merely unnamed? Frank did not know. Like others of his generation, he hoped that the vast waste of human life in the Great War had insured that it would be the war "to end all wars." What short of eternal peace could otherwise justify the carnage that had occurred on this continent? With each year, however, this lasting peace seemed less likely.

Fishing boats bobbed in the small bay.

As in Bayport . . .

There, his father had retired a year before from the insurance investigations business and had opened a hardware store that he called "Dixon & Sons," though one son had disappeared years before and the other remained resistant to Fenton Dixon's regular entreaties for him to return home to take his place in the new family business. How could he return to Bayport? Frank thought. All that awaited him there were parents who considered the last five years of his life a damnable waste of time (a consideration that had kept Frank himself awake at night even more than the music that drifted up to his flat from the *bal musette* across the street).

He stopped himself.

My life has not been wasted, he thought.

He had gained many dark and unexpected experiences working these years on the Left Bank. Sometimes, he tried to convey in letters the drama or pathos or comedy of these sordid incidents to his mother and father. But he had never managed, because he could never tell them about the real scent of opium smoldering within one or another of the dens he passed through in the Boulevard des Italiens (looking for a runaway heiress, perhaps, whom he might find prostrate on a velvet couch); nor could he ever adequately describe the sound of the jazz at Bricktop's, where the Negro bands from America played with an abandon he did not recall having heard in his collegiate excursions to New York City some years before.

Now, crossing the town square where merchants sold carnations and roses from carts, Frank planned his next hour or two. He would bathe and afterward read in his room at the Hôtel Royal, where at the Murphys' expense he had been enjoying accommodations far more comfortable than those he'd left behind on the Rue Servandoni. A private bath! Upon first seeing the airy hotel room he recalled F. Scott Fitzgerald's famous assertion, "The rich are different," to which Hemingway had allegedly responded: "Yes, Scott, they have more money than we do." Frank did not much like Hemingway, though Ernest was always polite to Frank when the two passed in Gertrude's *salon.* Frank wondered if his antipathy was the result of some reversal in his own guilty mind—wasn't it Frank who for years now had not only kept from Hemingway the secret of his long-missing suitcase but had also kept in the bottom drawer of his bureau the two "lost" short stories that had survived the theft? Was Frank's aversion to Hemingway merely a baroque self-justification? He preferred to account for his antipathy by considering as its source Ernest's callous dismissal of Hadley and their young son a year before—broad-shouldered Hadley, whose love had seemed so evident to Frank back in '23, before Hemingway became famous.

Frank continued toward the Hôtel Royal.

A bath and a book.

Frank was fond of a popular series of books by Maurice Leblanc about a cunning thief named Arsène Lupin, whose *sang-froid* and *savoir-faire,* as much as his strength and catlike physical agility, allowed him to give the slip to his corrupt pursuers, time and again. Frank liked that the thief responded in his adventures to a different moral authority than the mere law—as any good private investigator is likewise required to respond from time to time. For example, Frank himself had been guilty (technically) these past few years of breaking and entering, tampering with mail, burglary, petty theft, and even kidnapping. All in the pursuit of justice—or at least of setting things straight to somebody's semisatisfaction. He had found that real private investigations are rarely if ever inspired by the same innocent spirit that once inspired the hunting down of a lost will, the uncovering of a gang of smugglers, and the other local inquiries that Frank and Joe had undertaken together in Bayport years before. The Dixon boys—mere children then.

The hotel lobby was empty. Frank rang the bell on the desk.

In a matter of minutes, the stories of Arsène Lupin's heroic escapades would offer Frank respite from his thoughts. Some days, all he wanted from his life was to make it back to his room, close the door behind him, and open the latest Leblanc adventure for an hour or two. To breathe easy, safe in words. But when the clerk at the Hôtel Royal emerged to give Frank his room key and handed him a scribbled note as well, which Frank read as he started for the stairs, he became sufficiently distracted to forget Arsène Lupin, the gentleman burglar, altogether.

The note was from Jean-Paul, the local airplane mechanic:

Could Frank meet for a drink that evening in the Café du Monde? the note inquired. It seemed that Jean-Paul's cousin, to whom Frank's name had come up that afternoon, had shared a friendship in the war with a Joe Dixon of the 27th Aero Squadron. And he had also been a friend to Joe's wife, Genevieve.

Wife? Frank thought.

He wondered if the missing persons investigation that had brought him to Paris in the first place had just reopened.

Around midnight, the clouds parted and exposed a full moon that illuminated the shore for the first time since Carolyn Keene had slipped away from the Murphys' party. Now, sitting alone on the beach, her knees drawn to her chest, her back resting against a stone wall that rose to the sidewalk above, she saw before her the outline of a man. He stood on a patch of beach between the waterline and the wooden steps that led up to the Villa America, from which floated the improvisations of a jazz band and the indecipherable mix of words and shouts and laughter from the guests still engaged above. Carolyn could not see the face of the man. She knew he did not see her—his gaze was fixed in the opposite direction, out to sea. He paced a few steps at a time, betraying the slightest of limps. Carolyn thought of the hero of Scott Fitzgerald's latest novel, the gangster who gazed night after night over the Long Island Sound toward the green light at the end of his lover's boat dock. Carolyn looked away from the man's silhouette and toward where he looked. There, she saw nothing but a mist that hovered over the black Mediterranean.

Then a cloud covered the moon once more. The man's outline disappeared in the darkness.

She had not come here for company. Too many words had already been exchanged this night.

An hour before, in the parlor at the Murphys' party, Carolyn had overheard Hemingway chatting with his friend John Dos Passos, another writer. A mere, half-drunk reminiscence of Hemingway's youth in Oak Park, Illinois. Nonetheless, Carolyn could not help listening to him. Being in a room with Hemingway was like that. "This neighbor girl was a real beauty," he said. "Believe me, by the time she was a junior at Oak Park High School she knew what she had inside that little skirt of hers and she damn well intended to use it."

Carolyn sat across the room from Hemingway on a sofa with Pauline. They had retreated from the clamorous terrace for a quiet moment in which to gather their energies for what remained of the party outside.

"Of course this little tease wouldn't go with any of the local boys," Hemingway continued. "No, her sights were set higher than that. I was only a kid myself at the time, twelve or thirteen, but I'd have to have been a goddamn infant to miss the sway in her hips. I'd call that sway most 'ambitious.'" Unpleasant chatter, Carolyn thought, but no crueler than much of the gossip that circulated about the Quarter. At least Hemingway had no reason to believe that the girl in this story was known to anyone present. In this, however, he was wrong. "The sexy little bird's name was Anne Talbot," he said.

Carolyn looked across the room.

Hemingway could not have known his anecdote would mean something to Carolyn. After all, he did not know where Carolyn was born and raised. He did not know her father's occupation. He had intended no malice with his words. Nonetheless . . .

Anne Talbot, Oak Park. Four years older than Hemingway. Carolyn did the math in her head. Yes, the age was right and the hometown and the name. And the sexy sway in the walk, which Carolyn remembered from the first time she met Anne at a restaurant in Chicago. The sway had also been the last thing Carolyn saw of Anne, as she had watched her soon-to-be stepmother depart from Carolyn's darkened bedroom on that last night in River Heights. At times, Carolyn had suspected that there was no real Anne, but only a notable mode of walking.

However, there was a real Anne.

"Is something wrong, Carolyn?" Pauline asked.

"Oh, no."

"You seem distracted."

"No, no, just a little tired. Please, will you pour more coffee?"

Now—sitting alone on the dark beach—Carolyn wondered if Hemingway would have continued telling his story to Dos Passos if he had known that the out-of-town attorney, whose part in the developing tale was to be that of cheating husband, lascivious corrupter, and lovesick dupe, was the father of the young woman who at that moment sat across the room, well within listening distance. Would Hemingway have lowered his voice? Or would he have told the story even more loudly, watching as research for some future book the anguish on Carolyn's face? No matter. Carolyn was determined from the start that neither Hemingway nor anyone else would ever know what the anecdote meant to her.

"So, what about this girl?" Dos Passos asked in the Murphys' parlor.

Hemingway poured another drink from a bottle of gin left beside the bookshelf. Outside, the jazz band played "Ain't We Got Fun?" and dozens of shadows danced on the back wall of the room where Carolyn pretended to pay attention to Pauline's office gossip even as she followed Hemingway's words.

"Well, there was this attorney from River Heights," Hemingway said. "He was married at the time. But he'd visit Oak Park every few weeks, take Anne to the Flower Street Hotel for a night or two, and then go home to this quiet life where he was apparently the pillar of his community. He was happy. And Anne was happy too. Her affair proved to all the local boys that she was too good for them. It could have worked for a long time, a match made in heaven, except that the attorney's wife died in a train wreck. Made the papers. Anne read about it and immediately wanted to become the next Mrs. Attorney. See, until then, she'd told all her friends that the reason she hadn't married the guy was that she was averse to breaking up marriages. Especially when there was a kid involved. Now, with the wife gone, Anne made her play. But the attorney told her he had to devote all his attention to his daughter. No more nights in the hotel even. So Anne claimed to be pregnant. And the attorney panicked."

"What did he do?" Dos Passos asked.

"He gave her five thousand dollars to come to Paris on her own. Gave her the names of a few acquaintances to help her through 'the experience.' One of these acquaintances was a doctor. Of course, Anne wasn't pregnant. Still, she called on this doctor, just to give him the once-over. He was strictly an abortionist. Had some kind of potion that worked overnight. She pretended to take it. Then she wrote to the attorney in River Heights, distraught over the mortal sin she claimed to have committed. She told him she needed money to check herself into a sanitarium in Switzerland. When the money arrived, she went wild in the shops on the Champs-Elysées and set herself up in Passy as some kind of American heiress. When the money ran out, she wrote to River Heights for more. It went on like this for five years! Finally, the attorney cut her off. So guess what she did."

Dos Passos shrugged his shoulders.

"She returned to the States, first class on the *Mauretania,* and married him! Chased the daughter right out of the house. Last I heard, Anne and the attorney were living together in

River Heights, Mr. and Mrs. Respectable!"

Dos Passos laughed. "Happily ever after."

Hemingway took another swig. "Whatever works."

"How do you know all this?" Dos Passos asked.

"Hadley and I ran into Anne in Chicago back in '23. She looked damn good. We went to a speakeasy on Addison. She got tight and very chatty. Hadley was horrified. I thought it was funny as hell. Christ, she used to baby-sit me!"

"It's karma," Dos Passos said. "Those two being together now, every day."

"Karma?"

"Getting what you deserve."

"Oh, you mean the doling out of universal bullshit."

"Sure."

The men laughed.

About then, Carolyn vomited on the Murphys' lovely Persian rug. Hemingway and the others assumed she had been drinking too much. Pauline went to her. "Honey, honey, you need to lie down." Instead, Carolyn washed out her mouth with gin and slipped away alone. Eventually, she made her way down the Murphys' wooden steps, which led to the beach below.

Now, the clouds parted once more. The moon emerged.

"Are you all right, Miss?"

She looked up. The man from the shore stood not more than three feet away. In the moonlight, she saw his face. She recognized him, from somewhere. Had he been at the party? She scrambled to her feet, brushing the sand and wrinkles from her black dress. "How long have you been standing here?" she asked.

"Just a few seconds."

"Why?"

"I don't mean to bother you," he answered, "but you were sitting so still, for so long . . . I just wanted to make sure you were all right."

"I'm all right, thank you."

"Good."

He glanced up to the Murphys' crowded terrace. "You came out here to get some quiet?"

"Yes."

"I didn't mean to interrupt. I can leave you alone, if you'd like."

Carolyn had not come here for quiet alone. She had sought a place to hide. From Ernest and Pauline Hemingway. From the lovely Murphys. From Zelda's barbs and hard laughter. From Scott's self-destruction. And from all the others—what they knew of her, what they might want to know of her, what they might find out about her, what they might then say to one another about her next week over apéritifs. But this man did not seem to be one of them—inquisitive, manipulative, professionally clever. He had not asked, "What's wrong?" but only, "Are you all right?" A yes or no had been enough to retain his interest. Perhaps he did not see her as a model for a dissolute character in an as-yet-unwritten novel. Besides, she liked his face. And she had had enough of the insistent voices in her own head. She held out her hand. "My name is Carolyn."

"Frank," he said, taking her hand.

"I'm not at my best right now."

"You seem fine."

"Were you at the party?" she asked.

He shook his head. "I'm more an employee of the Murphys than a guest."

"Oh, what do you do?"

"I came down from Paris for the weekend to fly their plane."

"Is flying your profession?"

"No, I'm a private detective."

"A real one?"

He laughed. "I may not be a 'good' one, but I'm a 'real' one."

"'Real' is more important than 'good,'" she said.

"Well, I'm not a bad detective, either."

"No, of course not." She glanced toward the Murphys' terrace. "I was just thinking of them, up there."

"The Murphys?"

"All of them," she answered. "They're 'good' at what they do, whether it's painting or writing or dancing. Very, very good. But some of them aren't quite 'real' when it comes to who they are."

"One good thing about flying is that from up there, everybody down here's the same size, regardless of what they do."

"That makes sense."

"Everybody's just a little speck. But some specks . . ." He stopped.

"Yes?"

"This morning I noticed you from up there. You were raking the rocks from the beach with Gerald."

"And I was just a little speck?"

"Yes, but not just any speck."

"I'm afraid to fly."

"That's all right. Everybody's afraid of something."

"What are you afraid of, Mr. Flying Private Detective?"

"Plenty."

"For example?" she asked.

"Well, I . . ."

"Stop," she interrupted.

"What is it?"

"Don't answer my question."

"It's all right, I don't mind."

"No, please don't."

"Why not?"

"Because next you'll start asking me questions, and tonight I can say nothing about myself to you or to anyone, all right?"

"Okay."

She looked at the sea.

"Well, I'll leave you to your thoughts," he said.

"No, please." She turned back. "Don't do that. Not just yet. Tell me something happy."

He smiled. "Funny you should ask. Truth is, I got some very exciting news just a few hours ago."

"Yes?"

"A case I thought was closed has reopened."

"What sort of case?"

"A missing person."

"Did you find the missing person?"

"No, but I may."

"Man or woman?"

"A man. In fact, it's my . . ." He stopped.

"Who is it?"

"Would you like to hear a story?"

She nodded.

He took a deep breath. "Okay, once there was a fine young man named Joe Dixon who went off to war to fly airplanes with the 27th Aero Squadron. His big brother, let's call him Frank, stayed behind in the States. Joe was a damn good pilot, but disappeared from his squadron during an artillery attack. He may have been killed. He may have deserted. No one's ever known."

"So what did his brother do?"

"He left college, learned to fly, and eventually came to France where he opened a detective agency, specializing in missing persons. Years passed and Frank didn't find Joe. He began to fear he was wasting his life. After all, he had nothing to show for his efforts. And I don't just mean money. He feared he'd been a fool. Faithful, maybe. But that's all. And that's not really enough."

"Faithful seems pretty good to me," Carolyn said.

"Well, it's good. But by itself it's not enough."

"And tonight?"

Frank smiled. "Tonight I learned that Joe got married during his time here in France. I'd never known. A girl named Genevieve. Of course, it was against regulations for aviators to marry local girls, and so Joe couldn't tell us in his letters, which were censored. This isn't boring you, is it?"

"No, not at all."

"I've talked to dozens of men over the years who flew with Joe. They all said he was a good flyer, a natural, but they never seemed to know much about what his off-hours had been like. I worried that maybe he'd been lonely here. Of course, now I understand why his comrades knew nothing. Joe had a secret."

"And when you find her, you may find him?"

Frank nodded.

"And then what?" she asked.

"Then my life will be my own, I think."

"Ah, what a prospect," she said. Few people could make such a claim, she thought. Surely not herself. She looked away. The sky had almost cleared and the Mediterranean shimmered white in the moonlight. From here, the distant revelers on the Murphys' crowded terrace were mere glittering flashes of color, moving to the sound of jazz.

"Would you like to walk together?" he asked.

She did not answer him. Instead: "When I was a girl, we lived in a white house with a green porch that ran along all four sides," she said. "I used to imagine that one day a flood would dislodge our house from its foundation and we would float down the river and onto the sea. The green porch would be like a ship's deck, which I could stroll during the sunny hours, and my room on the second floor would be like a stateroom from which I could look out and see the whole world passing by."

"Go on," he said.

"When my mother died, I thought the ship had sunk. But it hadn't. Not yet at least."

She stopped. Why was she telling him this?

"Would you like to take a walk?" he asked again.

She shook her head.

"I promise I won't ask you any questions," he added.

"I work at *Vogue* magazine." She rummaged through her purse before handing him a business card. "Call me at this number if you'd like to go for a walk some other time, when we're back in Paris. I'll be more myself in a few days."

"Carolyn Keene," he read, before slipping the card into his pocket.

"You seem nice, Frank."

"Thank you."

She turned and started up the weathered, wobbly stairs to the boardwalk above. She would not return to the Villa America, she thought. She would find a hotel and send for her bags in the morning. *Le Train Bleu* left for Paris at eight-thirty. Perhaps Frank would call her. She hoped so. When she reached the top of the stairs she turned back and looked down to the beach.

There Frank remained.

She had half expected him to be a hallucination.

PART TWO

Paris
(three weeks later)

The waters were very swift at this point, for the
current was strong and the river was deep.

Franklin W. Dixon
The Secret of the Old Mill

The first night Frank spent with Carolyn on her creaky houseboat, holding her in his arms on her narrow bed, a driving rain caused the Seine to roll in gentle swells beneath them. All seemed to move as one—he, she, the river.

Now it was after midnight.

"If the boat comes unmoored," Carolyn whispered, "we may find by morning that we've floated downriver to the sea and from there, well . . . to anywhere."

"That would be fine," Frank said.

"Fine to float anywhere at all?"

He pulled her closer, her body warm and soft and smooth in his arms. "Anywhere."

These past weeks, Frank and Carolyn had walked together most mornings along the Rue Servandoni to the Boulevard St-Germain for coffee and brioche. In the afternoons they strolled, hand in hand, along the quays where among the shuttered bookstalls they found American novels for sale very cheap. In the evenings they crossed the river to walk the narrow streets of the Ile St-Louis, admiring the old, tall houses. Though Frank's Yankee upbringing had made him uncomfortable with sentimental notions like a *coup de foudre* (love at first sight, sudden and powerful as a bolt of lightning) he knew he had been struck.

He had never been happier.

Nonetheless, his return to Paris had not been without frustration. Frank's most pressing and personal investigation (the search for Joe's wife, who he had learned in Antibes was named Genevieve Dufour) now promised little hope of resolution. In 1918, just after Joe took leave of his squadron and the rest of the world, Genevieve too had disappeared. Frank was a professional, his specialty: missing persons, *les disparus,* etc. Nonetheless, Genevieve Dufour Dixon remained as unaccounted for as her long-lost husband, despite Frank's best efforts. Hadn't he tracked down dozens of runaways, heiresses, embezzlers, and missing spouses? Routine. Why then had finding either Joe or Genevieve proven much more difficult? he wondered.

The question haunted him.

Even happiness could not keep it from rattling about his head.

"Are you thinking detective thoughts?" Carolyn asked, cuddled in his arms.

"How did you know?"

"You have many different ways of being silent," she answered.

"You're not a bad detective yourself," he observed.

Two weeks before, he had begun his search for Genevieve by traveling to her hometown, Reims. There, he learned that her three brothers had been killed at the Battle of the Marne, that her father had died of a brain seizure shortly thereafter, and that her mother Jeanne-Marie now collected a pension but was months behind on her municipal taxes. The street where Genevieve Dufour grew up and where her mother still lived wound through a working-class quarter. Frank counted off the numbers on the row of plaster-and-timber flats along Genevieve's street—*cent-deux, cent-quatre.* He stopped at *cent-six,* which stood near the middle of the block.

He knocked.

After a long time, Jeanne-Marie Dufour—white-haired, bent about the shoulders, and wearing a faded dress more suited to the *Belle Epoch* than to this age of lithe lines—opened the door.

"Madame Dufour?" Frank asked, still full of hope.

"Yes?"

"My name is Frank Dixon. My brother was married to your daughter."

"The American?" she asked.

He nodded.

"The deserter," she said.

"The war did strange things to good people," Frank said.

"I'm not speaking now of his military obligations," she interrupted.

"Oh."

"You are quite brave to come here, Monsieur Dixon. If my husband were alive he'd shoot you in place of your brother."

"Then your daughter did not go away with my brother when he disappeared?"

She laughed. "No, he went away without her."

"I'm sorry. I didn't know. I was hoping . . ."

"Yes?"

"Well, I only learned last week about Joe's marriage to your daughter. I thought, perhaps . . ."

"Marriage?" she interrupted. "A secret wedding, a honeymoon, and an abandonment do not make a marriage. And that is all they ever had, do you understand? They never lived together, really."

"I'm just trying to learn what happened."

She said nothing but stepped away from the doorway and motioned for Frank to follow her inside.

"Thank you, Madame."

She led him through the entry to the tiny parlor; there, thick drapes covered the only window. Light came from a gas lantern set on a table beside a rose in a vase. On a wall hung three black-ribboned photographs of Madame Dufour's lost sons.

"Do you want to sit?" she asked.

"Thank you."

"Where is your brother these days?"

"I don't know. I've heard nothing from him since 1918."

"That is a long time—perhaps he is dead."

"Perhaps."

"Why have you learned only now about your brother's marriage? Were you not close to him?"

"We were close."

"Then why did he not trust you with the news?"

"Marriage was against Air Corps regulations. Joe had no choice but to keep it secret."

"If your own brother did not trust you, then why should I?"

"Oh, he trusted me."

"So you say."

"I'm sure he wanted me to know. But his letters were censored by the military."

"So, what do you want from me?"

"I want to know about your daughter, Genevieve."

The old woman claimed to know nothing about her daughter's life since 1918. Her relationship with Genevieve had been terminated at the time of the girl's elopement, the news of which had so enraged Genevieve's father—already half mad from the recent deaths of his sons—that he disowned the girl, wishing her only misery in her new life in Paris with "l'américain." Within months of her departure, Monsieur Dufour was dead. It had been no seizure. Rather, he had dashed out his own brains with a brick from the back stoop near the dustbin. He had lain among the ashes for a long time, blood and tissue oozing from a hole the size of a twenty-franc coin in his skull. Madame Dufour explained that the city authorities were concerned that she not be stigmatized by the scandal of a suicide in her family—as if she could still care about such things! All was lost to her. Including her daughter, who by then was no longer to be found in Paris.

"Perhaps I will find her," Frank said.

"To what end?"

"To ask her a few questions about my brother."

"And what makes you think she knew him any better than you did?"

"Perhaps not better," he answered. "But she knew him during a period of his life that I've been unable to understand."

"And if she had nothing to say to you?"

"Then it would be only me, speaking to her."

"And what would you say?"

"I would tell her I was sorry."

In the days that followed, Frank interviewed those of Genevieve's girlhood friends who still lived in and about

Reims. From them, he constructed an understanding of Genevieve that neither her mother's recollections nor the photographs in the family album could provide.

Genevieve had been a spirited and happy girl.

But the war changed everything.

The Marne, the Argonne Forest—locales that became synonymous with death. One local boy dead, then another and another. Then the catastrophe—her own brothers. Genevieve wore no ribbons to commemorate her lost brothers' heroism. Rather, she raged through the streets, shouting that she would kill with her father's rifle the next Frenchman who spoke to her of patriotism or glory. When neighbors offered consolation, she turned on them with such anger that even now they remembered her expression as one of the most frightening sights of the war years. Only the parish priest dared reproach the girl; in response, she announced to him that she no longer believed in God, though she was convinced that Satan was real. Then she disappeared into her family's home and did not emerge for more than two months.

Afterward, the airfield and an American flyer.

None of Genevieve's friends ever met Joe Dixon, but all had heard her stories about him. Genevieve and Joe met in a café where Joe had gone to celebrate shooting down two Fokkers in a dogfight over Pont-à-Mousson. No one in Reims could recall what Genevieve had said about their first conversations. There was probably little to recall. She had studied English with only passing marks. And Joe's use of French was limited to his perusal of a noun out of the French/English dictionary he had bought upon his arrival at Le Havre. Even so, vocabulary proved no obstacle for the two, whose first rendezvous in a barn on a summer night Genevieve recalled to friends as having been idyllic. When

Joe was reprimanded by his commanding officer for absences from the air base, he responded by becoming even more devoted to Genevieve. When he was grounded for three days, the two secretly married, though Genevieve remained in her father's home. Two months later, during a leave of absence, Joe took his wife away to settle her in the Luxembourg Quarter.

Here, the recollections of Genevieve's friends ended.

Frank thought his investigations in Reims had likewise come to an end. But background information is never wasted, he believed; understanding a missing person's character and history is often as important as discovering contemporary contacts, occupations, or even addresses. To those in Reims, Genevieve had seemed to disappear; to Frank, she was just becoming discernible. Then a voice on the train platform minutes before the arrival of the express to Paris:

"Monsieur Dixon?"

He turned. Madame Dufour stood an arm's length away, having pressed through a crowd of travelers.

"I have something to tell you," she said.

"Oh?"

"My sister, God rest her soul, happened across Genevieve in Paris at the end of the war. There, she learned something that you should know."

"Yes?"

"Genevieve married another man a few weeks after your brother's disappearance."

"What?"

"I know nothing more about her life after that, Monsieur Dixon."

"Remarried after a few weeks?"

"Do not be offended, Monsieur Dixon."

"No, no."

"Genevieve must have believed she would not be welcomed back in my home. She must have felt alone. But I would not have turned her away. Oh, think of her in that city, where your brother was so anxious to abandon her. He had no right to take her away from here."

"Why did you not tell me this before?"

"Because I was afraid of what you might learn about my daughter."

"You mean that I might find her?"

She nodded.

"Don't you want to see her again, Madame Dufour?" he asked.

"Everyone in my life dies, Monsieur Dixon. I do not believe that you could ever bring me news of Genevieve that is different from the news I received of her brothers or father. I feel in my heart that she is gone. Why should I want to know it as well as feel it?"

"Because she might be alive."

"Wouldn't she have contacted me by now?"

"Maybe. But isn't knowing, one way or the other, better than not knowing?"

"Not necessarily," she said.

"Then why have you told me now?"

"Because I do not hate you as I hate your brother. I do not want you to waste your life looking for a Genevieve Dixon when no woman by such a name exists anymore. She is called something else now."

"What is her husband's name?"

She said nothing.

"Do you know?" he asked.

She nodded.

"Well?"

"I said I did not want you to waste your life, Monsieur Dixon. I did not say I wanted you to find my daughter."

She turned to go.

"Wait."

She stopped.

"What if I promise never to tell you what I learn, Madame Dufour? Will you give me her name then?"

"I will think on it. Do not contact me again. I will write you with my decision."

Then she was gone.

A telegram from Madame Dufour had arrived earlier this evening as Frank was preparing to leave his apartment to come here to Carolyn's houseboat. Madame Dufour's words were scripted in a flowery hand that seemed a dramatic contrast to her austere figure. *Abandonnez l'espoir,* she had written. Abandon hope—as if her message was to be posted above the entrance to hell. Nothing more. Frank balled the note and tossed it across the room. For a few minutes he did not move. Then he returned to the washbasin to finish shaving; next, he combed his hair, knotted his tie, and then started toward the Seine and his rendezvous with Carolyn as if nothing had happened.

But something had happened.

Twenty minutes later, he arrived at the edge of the Seine near the Pont Neuf. On the river floated a dozen wooden houseboats, each about thirty feet long, most hung with drying laundry on their decks, all chained to iron rings rusted into the stone walls along the Seine. Carolyn's was the barge with the potted flowers on deck. Frank recalled a line from Scott Fitzgerald's latest novel: " . . . boats against the current, borne ceaselessly into the past."

He crossed from the quay to the deck of the leaky old tub.

Now, hours later with Carolyn in his arms, he thought that if the houseboat were to spring a leak and sink into the Seine he would not resist the embrace of the swirling river as it engulfed him; rather, he would close his eyes and whisper Carolyn's name.

He would never abandon her, he thought.

What had come over Joe all those years before?

"Carolyn," he whispered.

"Yes?"

"When I first came to France I believed Joe was alive and that I'd not only find him but would also learn of some honorable reason he had abandoned those who counted on him."

She turned to him on the narrow bed. "And now, Frank?"

"I don't think he's alive anymore."

"I'm sorry."

"But that's not the worst of it," he said.

"What's worse?"

"There've been times these past years when I think I wanted more to discover an honorable brother, even if he was dead, than a dishonorable one who was alive."

She said nothing.

"That's the worst," he continued. "My own brother, whom I love."

She touched his face. "How could you not be discouraged from time to time?"

"It's not just discouragement. It's shame and cowardice."

"But that's not you."

"It's me sometimes, when I'm crazy."

"Well, everybody's crazy sometimes," she said.

Yes, Frank thought. Just the week before he had noted the following in his journal:

I must be crazy! Last night Carolyn came back with me to my apartment and asked to read one of my short stories (we had discussed our writing at dinner). I agreed, forgetting for a moment that I've never actually completed any of the goddamn things. Beginnings, middles, and nothing more . . . I opened the desk drawer and withdrew a manuscript, which felt meager in my hand. Was this the best I had to show Carolyn Keene, who socializes with the likes of F. Scott Fitzgerald? One unfinished work after another . . . What does such incompletion say about me? "Well?" Carolyn pressed as I lingered over the drawer. So I withdrew the two typed, unsigned Hemingway stories that I salvaged years ago from the lost suitcase and have kept hidden ever since. "Here're a couple of stories I wrote a long time ago," I said, handing them to her. With Carolyn's first words of praise I felt a wave of regret. But by then what could I do? Yes, crazy. Worse than crazy.

Since then, Frank had fended off Carolyn's suggestions that he possessed secret talent as an author. Yet, he had discovered no moment in that time that he was willing to spoil by confessing to such a stupid lie.

Surely, not this moment.

Besides, mightn't his deception prove in the end as harmless as the self-protective yarns he had spun years before as a schoolboy (wherein the thickened sole of his "special" shoe contained secret government papers or nitroglycerin)?

"So, you've done crazy things too?" he asked.

She nodded. "When I was nine years old I attempted to walk all the way around the world. Is that crazy enough for you?"

"Well, it's ambitious."

"I really attempted it. Step by step."

He laughed. "Why?"

"My parents had taken me to a carnival," she said. "After I got off a carousel, my father asked my mother and me if we knew in which direction we'd find our house. Just a game. My mother pointed one way and I pointed another. 'Well, Dad, which is it?' I asked. 'Who's right and who's wrong?' I felt so damn sure of myself."

"Which direction was it?"

"My father pointed the same way as my mother. He laughed, all very good-natured. My mother wasn't even paying attention to the game anymore."

"But your father was wrong?"

"No, he was right. So was my mother. As soon as he pointed, I realized I'd gotten turned around in the carnival."

"That happens."

"Sure, but I refused to admit I was wrong. Instead, I slipped away from them in a crowd. It was easy. And I set off walking in the direction I'd pointed, because the world is round and I knew that if I walked long enough I'd end up being right."

He laughed. "You were an ambitious child."

"Stubborn is more like it," she said. "I was angry when the police brought me back. See, I still believed I could have made it all the way around, if I'd been left to my own devices. And I was downright furious with my mother, because I thought she was glad I'd been proven wrong. That's crazy, huh? What was wrong with me?"

"You were just a kid."

"Sure, but being a kid was all the time I ever had with my mother. In those days, I never considered that she had grownup feelings and problems."

Frank knew Carolyn's mother had died years before. He knew also that her lingering anger toward her father had something to do with her parents' marriage, though Carolyn was reluctant to reveal details. She too had secrets, he thought. "I'm sure your mother never felt shortchanged by you," he said.

"I didn't feel shortchanged by her."

"She'd be proud of you."

Carolyn shrugged. "Here I am, halfway around the world. She'd probably think I was still trying to make it all the way around."

"Are you?"

"Maybe."

Frank's words escaped his lips before he had time to temper them with a prudent lover's caution. "Can I come with you the rest of the way?"

"Frank, Frank. You are crazy."

What did that mean? he wondered. "We're good company, right?" he suggested.

"Yes, but it's a long way around the whole world."

"Good."

She smiled. "Which direction do you want to go?"

"Doesn't matter," he said. "Round and round is okay with me."

A Visit from Home

. . .his eyes held her attention, for in expression they were sad, almost tragic.

Carolyn Keene
The Secret at Shadow Ranch

Carolyn Keene left Frank's apartment on the Rue Servandoni almost an hour before she was due across the river at the Ritz bar, where, according to the telegram she had received from Italy, she was to meet her father and stepmother for drinks and "catching up." Carolyn had not seen her father since she left River Heights six years before; in that time they had exchanged only cursory correspondence. It was three months now since she had learned in Cap d'Antibes of his betrayal of her mother.

More than miles and time separated them.

Mr. and Mrs. Keene indicated in their wire that they had only two hours to spare for the visit, as their express train would be leaving Paris at three o'clock for Calais. Not even an entire day, Carolyn thought—as if Paris were a mere railroad hub! She was almost as disturbed by her father's dismissal of her adopted city as she was by what seemed his dismissal of her. At first, she considered wiring to Italy that she would be unavailable during those two hours—or any two hours. But she hadn't the heart to deny their visit. Starting down the stairs of Frank's building and out onto the busy street, however, she was no longer sure.

She missed Frank, who had left the apartment only a few minutes before.

His apartment. Their apartment.

A fortnight before, Carolyn's rusted and weathered houseboat had sprung a leak. Frank and she had transported her possessions from the boat to the quay and then on to his apartment. That first night they had made love in his bedroom, which was now piled high with her possessions—the bed was the only space wide enough to accommodate their thrashings, though at one point they rolled off the mattress and onto a scattering of her books, which pressed hard against her spine but smelled deliciously of leather bindings and old pages. When she closed her eyes she imagined lush, inky words floating all about her. In the days that followed, tradesmen indicated that the boat was no longer worth repairing; as a result, Carolyn and a few of her boxed possessions had taken temporary residence with Jeanne Morestal, a friend from the magazine who owned a house in the 11th arrondissement. However, most of Carolyn's nights continued to be spent with Frank; she felt more at home in his far-too-small flat on the Rue Servandoni than she wished to admit, even to herself.

Why, then, had she insisted she go to the Ritz alone? she wondered now.

Under ordinary circumstances she'd have been happy for Frank to meet her father—or at least to meet the Carson Keene she had thought she knew as a girl. And she'd be proud for this same upstanding father to meet Frank. But these were not ordinary circumstances (she was no longer sure that "ordinary circumstances" existed for anyone). She tried to explain as much to Frank the night before, without admitting to the real source of her reticence—her own confused rage regarding her father's adultery. "Just trust me, Frank," she said amid the night bustle of Les Halles, where they had gone for a late dinner of *soupe à l'oignon, escargots,* and *boudin.*

"Okay," he said.

Now, crossing the river at the Pont Royal, Carolyn wondered where Frank might be. Was he sitting beneath one of the wooden Chinese statues in Les Deux Magots café handicapping the daily racing form, his penciled marks across the newsprint as indecipherable to her as Arabic characters? Or had he settled back in his chair on the sidewalk outside Les Deux Magots with an Arsène Lupin novel? Or was he talking to one of his informants, who worked for anisette and five-franc coins, or talking to a client, who might be searching for a lost fortune, a lost *objet d'art*, a lost wife? Maybe he was thinking about Carolyn herself, wondering where she was just now—wondering if she was thinking about him.

A nice possibility, she thought.

She stopped beside the giant obelisk at the center of the Place Vendôme and looked across the square to the granite entrance of the Ritz, which was guarded by two doormen in uniforms as trim as those of Napoleon's personal guard. She glanced at her wristwatch, surprised to discover how much time had passed since she'd left St-Germain des Prés. She remembered nothing of her walk here. Not a single street crossing, not an automobile, not another pedestrian, not the Seine, not the Tuileries, not the lovely but too-expensive stores on this side of the river. She passed through the entrance, the liveried doormen cold and officious.

The lobby was thick with quiet. Her heart pounded.

The bar was almost empty. Not empty.

Mr. and Mrs. Keene sat in the far corner drinking from tiny glasses of liqueur. Carolyn saw the two before they saw her. Her father looked far older than she remembered. Gray streaked his mustache, bags puffed beneath his eyes, his shoulders seemed to have shrunk. (Or was it possible that this most fastidious of dressers was wearing a jacket that had been tailored improperly?) Anne seemed not to have changed. Except perhaps that her skin was even whiter, more perfect. And her fingers sparkled now with rings. How could she be somebody's mother? Carolyn wondered.

Then they saw her and there was no getting away.

"Carolyn!" Carson Keene called, standing.

"Hello, Dad," she answered, stepping into the bar.

"Carolyn, Carolyn," he repeated.

She walked toward him, disarmed by his wide, genuine grin.

Meantime, Anne smiled up at her. "Hello, dear girl."

Carson Keene opened his arms; he pulled Carolyn in. "Where have you been, my sweet?" he asked.

She kissed his cheek, then stepped away and looked at her watch. "I'm not late, am I?" she asked.

"No, no, silly," he answered. "I mean, where've you been all of these years."

"Where indeed?" Anne said, standing and taking Carolyn's hand.

"I've been here," Carolyn answered.

"The Ritz bar?" Anne joked.

"In Paris, I mean," Carolyn said. "All these years."

"Sit down, dear," Anne said, sitting down.

"What'll you have to drink?" Carson asked as the waiter appeared.

"Bring me a *vin blanc*," she said.

The waiter disappeared.

"Well, well, here we are," Carson said. "I was worried that you might be out of town or something. Sorry about the short notice, Carolyn, but this whole trip was a last-minute, whirlwind sort of endeavor."

Anne nodded. "Impetuosity is delightful, don't you think, Carolyn?"

None of it felt real to Carolyn. Not the two seated before her, not the bar, not the granite building about them or the city of Paris outside. Even the air she breathed seemed false. She thought that if she closed her eyes right now and then opened them she would discover herself sitting up in her bed, having dreamt the whole thing.

"Impetuosity keeps us young," Anne said.

"Well, one of you is young," Carolyn answered.

"Ouch," Carson said, smiling. He tried to catch his daughter's eye. She looked away. "It's all just a state of mind, anyway, Carolyn," he said. "Youth, old age, et cetera."

"Absolutely," Anne pronounced, stretching the single word to the duration of a long sentence.

"Well, here we are . . ." Carson said.

"Not all of us," Carolyn answered. She thought of Frank.

Carson smiled. "Ah, yes, little Rose. Oh, she's a beauty. Like you, Carolyn. And her mother here, of course. You'll love her."

"Yes, the baby," Anne said. "I brought you a picture, my dear, but I forgot it upstairs. We'll get it before we leave, all right?"

"She's not really a baby anymore, is she?" Carolyn asked.

"She's almost five," Anne answered. "She starts school in September. Can you believe it?"

"Amazing!" Carson added.

"Yes, it's amazing," Anne murmured. "Truly, truly."

"Don't all children her age start school in September?" Carolyn asked.

Anne laughed. "Of course."

"What we mean is that it's amazing how big she's gotten," her father said.

"She's very big for her age?" Carolyn asked.

He drained his tiny glass.

"Oh Carolyn, always kidding," Anne said.

"Maybe when I see her picture I'll understand everything," Carolyn said.

The waiter arrived.

"Your drink's here, Carolyn," Carson said. He turned to the waiter. "Bring me a whiskey."

The waiter turned to Anne. "Madame?" he asked.

Anne crossed her hands like a schoolgirl on the table before her. "Oh, I'm fine, Monsieur. *Merci.*"

They all watched the waiter go, as if his leaving was of interest.

"Look, it's been a long time, Carolyn," Carson said. "We're sorry about that."

"Yes," she answered.

"But the one good thing about all the years that have passed is that now we're adults," he continued. "All of us. We can approach the world as adults. We can understand each other as adults. Carolyn, you were an adult at age eight, if I recall properly."

"Actually, I wasn't."

He tried to smile. "Well, you acted like it."

"Thank you, I guess."

"You're welcome," he said. "I mean it as a compliment. What a remarkable little woman you were, Carolyn. Running our household. Or at least acting like you were running it."

"Your father's missed you very much," Anne said. "We've both missed you."

"That's nice," Carolyn said.

"Isn't it fine being together again?" Carson asked.

"Yes, but . . ." Carolyn stopped.

"But what?" Carson asked.

"Well, if it strikes you as being so 'fine,' Dad, then what's your big hurry to get to England? I mean, two hours in Paris?"

"We are sorry about that," Carson said. "Damn boat schedules."

"And train schedules too," Anne added. "Hotel reservations. The whole 'tour' concept is very complicated. All the coordination involved. If you miss one connection, you've missed them all."

The waiter brought the whiskey.

Carson drank.

No one spoke.

Later, Carolyn wondered if they would ever have spoken again had Scott Fitzgerald not walked into the bar at that moment. She wondered if they might all have sat silent for the next hour, sipping drinks, nodding occasional orders to the waiter for refills, glancing from time to time at their wristwatches (Anne's sparkling of gold) for promises of imminent release. Would they have become as mummified in their places as Professor Carter's latest archaeological discoveries in Egypt?

"Oh, look," Carolyn said. "A friend of mine." She waved across the room.

"Is that . . . ?" Anne asked.

"Yes," Carolyn said.

"Well, my goodness," Anne whispered. "You really know him?"

"Hello, Carolyn, how are you?" Scott said.

Everyone stood for introductions.

"Please join us," Carson suggested.

The four sat.

"Where's Zelda?" Carolyn asked.

"Dance lessons," he answered, before ordering a gin from the waiter.

"What a delightful form of exercise," Anne said.

"To my wife it's much more than just exercise," Scott said. "It's her reason for being, these days."

Anne laughed.

"I don't exaggerate," Scott continued. "She intends to become a prima ballerina with the Ballet Russe. Of course, she didn't start dancing until she was twenty-eight. You have to admire such courage, right? Or whatever word you want to use to describe it."

"Absolutely," Anne said.

"She intends to make up with determination for what she lacks in experience and flexibility and, well, youth," he said. "Youth, the irreplaceable quality."

"My father says that age is just a state of mind," Carolyn said.

Scott turned to Carson. "Do you believe that?"

"Of course not," Carson answered, laughing.

"Oh, I've read about Zelda's wild dancing for years," Anne said. "You can't fool me, Scott. Dancing's nothing new for Zelda. Or for you. I know all about it."

Scott shrugged. "The Charleston doesn't count."

Anne laughed. "Ah, yes! And dancing in the fountain outside the Plaza Hotel."

"Oh, right," he said. "Well, yes, that little incident was some time ago now."

"Good for Mrs. Fitzgerald," Carson said. "I mean the ballet dancing. She's got gumption."

Scott nodded. "It gets her up in the morning."

"We all need something," Carson said.

"Yes, and she's begun a novel of her own too."

"Sounds like there's plenty going on in that head of hers," Anne said.

"More than you could ever imagine," Scott answered.

"We're sorry not to have met her," Carson said.

"How's your new book coming?" Carolyn asked.

He shrugged.

"I loved *This Side of Paradise*," Anne said. "What an admirable main character!"

The waiter delivered Scott's gin.

"Amory Blaine?" Scott asked. "He's an egotistic boob, don't you think?"

"Well, he's an egotist, surely," she answered. "I mean, the book calls him an egotist right from the beginning. Nothing wrong with that. But a boob?"

"Trust me," Scott said. "He's a boob. Even if half the world was fooled by him."

"Well, you're the author," she said.

"Yes, and I'm also Amory Blaine." He laughed and took a drink. "Which, I suppose, makes you part of the half that's been fooled, my dear Mrs. Keene!"

Anne grinned and touched him playfully on the shoulder.

"You have to be careful not to be left behind, Mrs. Keene," he continued. "You must remember that the number of readers I fool has been dwindling in recent years. Heed my warning, my dear. I'd hate for you to discover yourself the last reader in America still holding one of my books in your zealous little hands. You'd feel so . . . lonely."

She laughed again. "You're joking, of course."

"You're still the most famous writer in America," Carson said, as if Fitzgerald might not keep track of such things.

"He's just having a bad day with his new book," Carolyn said.

"You're right," Scott admitted. "The book's not going well. Of course, it'll come out all right in the end, whatever it turns out to be."

"What's your new book called?" Anne asked.

"It's called *The Boy Who Killed His Mother.*"

"Oh?"

"It's only a working title."

"Very interesting," Carson said.

"Of course, your daughter is not fond of all my titles," Scott confided to Carson.

"What do you mean?" Carolyn interrupted. "I love your books."

"I'm talking about their titles," he said. "Don't you remember?"

Carolyn laughed. "I was hoping you'd forgotten."

"Last year she told me *The Great Gatsby* sounded like the name of a magician," he continued.

"I haven't had the pleasure of reading that one yet," Anne said.

"Don't worry, Mrs. Keene," Scott answered. "You're in a vast company of those who haven't read that one yet."

"We middle westerners do our best to keep up with things," Carson interjected. "Maybe not like folks here in Paris or over in New York but . . ."

"You don't have to convince me, Mr. Keene," Scott interrupted. "I'm a middle westerner myself."

"Of course," Carson said. "I spotted it right away."

"You know, Scott, you're not the first famous author I've met," Anne said.

As if Scott could care, Carolyn thought.

"When I was a girl in Oak Park I actually used to babysit Ernest Hemingway, another of your expatriates here. Do you know him?"

"What! I discovered him!" Scott said.

Anne. Oak Park. Hemingway.

The whole story was true.

Carolyn stood up.

"What is it?" Carson asked. "Is something wrong?"

"Are you all right, Carolyn?" Scott asked.

She could not listen to Anne talk about her youth in Oak Park.

"Dear, your face," Anne said. "You look like you've seen a ghost."

"I just need some air," Carolyn said.

"Are you all right?" her father repeated.

"Yes, yes." She started out of the bar.

"Carolyn?" he called.

She moved through the lobby and onto the sidewalk.

Outside, the Place Vendôme bustled. She was glad for the noise. She wished the smoke from the diesel buses and the cars would become thick enough to obscure the air and provide her shelter into which she might disappear. She stopped at the edge of the sidewalk. Then she heard her name. She turned.

Her father had followed her outside.

He was alone.

"Carolyn, are you all right?"

"How could you!" Carolyn said.

"How could I what?"

"Betray my mother."

"I don't know what you're talking about."

She said nothing.

"Maybe you don't know what you're talking about, Carolyn," he said. "Maybe you're wrong. Have you considered that?"

"Yes, I've considered it. Endlessly."

"Well," he said. "What happened was strictly between your mother and me."

"And Anne."

"How do you know this?"

"That doesn't matter."

"It was a long time ago. And it had nothing to do with you, Carolyn."

"Of course it did."

"Of course it didn't," he said. "I owe you no explanations. I only owe your mother, Carolyn, and she can't hear me anymore."

Carolyn said nothing.

"Besides," he continued. "You're not angry with me just because I was unfaithful to her."

"No?"

"You're angry with me because you believe I betrayed you."

Yes, she thought.

"And maybe I did betray you," he said. "But I never wanted to, Carolyn. For whatever that's worth. For years I twisted my own life, and my values, to keep from having to compromise the life I wanted for you. The beautiful girlhood that you must remember! It didn't come without cost. Do you think keeping secrets all those years was fun? Do you think I didn't toss and turn every night trying to conceive ways of containing all the damage I was wreaking? Christ, I deceived Anne in those days as cruelly as I ever deceived your mother."

"You weren't married to Anne."

"That's true, but she was only a girl."

Carolyn turned away.

"Believe me," he said. "I behaved shamefully. Whatever you heard about me—well, I'm sure I was worse. Falling in love with Anne . . . I can never explain that. It just happened. Your mother didn't deserve it. She was a good woman. Maybe if things had been different between her and me. Don't get me wrong, I'm not blaming her, but . . ."

"But the lies," she said. "And all that's happened since."

"I did what I did to protect what we had," he said. "Our family of two. Believe me, I fought for your happy girlhood until the last moment, when I could no longer . . ."

"No longer what?"

"When Anne could no longer be ignored in your favor," he said. "That's right. I owed her something too. I couldn't deny it any longer. She wouldn't let me. It had been years. And she was right. Still, I almost made it, Carolyn. I almost got you through school—maybe off to college. Almost got you to *happy*. But I didn't, and I know that all the years that came before crashed down on you because at the end I failed. Do you think I don't know that? Do you think I haven't missed you?"

"How could I know what to think?"

"You could have asked."

"No."

"I raised a very proud girl."

She nodded.

"Of course, even if you had asked, I'd have lied," he said, looking away. "Even after our life together in River

Heights was in ruins and you went away, I didn't want you to know the truth about me. All these years I've justified the distance between us by imagining that what you needed most in your life was a father you could admire. But that was a lie. I understand that now. The truth, Carolyn, since you're asking for it, is that what I needed most in my own life was to be admired. I pushed you away in hopes of satisfying my needs, not yours, however I may have attempted to rationalize my weakness, and I have suffered for those selfish, futile decisions every single day. Is that enough truth for you?"

"It's been so many years," she said.

"There's a part of me you know very well," he said. "Better than anyone."

"And another part I can never know."

"That's true."

She turned away. "That's always the case with those we love, isn't it?" she said.

"I don't know."

"I've met a man," she said.

"Good."

"And I care about him a lot."

"Okay."

"But love disappears, doesn't it?"

"Not necessarily."

"When it goes, where does it go?" she asked. "That's all I've ever wanted to know. It's not so much to ask. If only I knew the answer to that one question, then I could live with the fact that it has to go away in the first place. Otherwise, it's just cruel."

He looked at her a long time. "Carolyn, love may not have to—"

A voice: "Carson?"

He stopped at the sound of Anne's voice.

She had emerged from the hotel.

He turned.

Carolyn watched her father look at Anne. She watched Anne look back at him.

Neither bore for the other a kind expression.

"That Fitzgerald fellow is more interested in his gin and tonic than in talking about American literature with me," Anne said, starting toward them. "Actually, he's a bit of a disappointment, in person."

That evening, long after Mr. and Mrs. Carson Keene departed for Calais, Carolyn made her way back across the river to Frank's apartment.

Frank waited for her inside.

"How did it go?" he asked.

She stood before him, saying nothing.

"Carolyn? What is it? What happened?"

"Whatever you are, Frank, is all right with me," she said. "Whatever happens, happens. Because humans are just human. But don't lie to me, Frank."

"Never, Carolyn," he said.

An Unexpected Turn

*They felt particularly carefree and never
dreamed of the news they were to hear or
of how it was to affect them and
their chums.*

Franklin W. Dixon
The Missing Chums

Two weeks later, Frank strolled with Carolyn beside his
friend Gertrude Stein, who walked behind the straining
leash of her little dog, on a gravel path in the Luxembourg
Gardens. Their plan had originally been to spend the afternoon at 27 Rue de Fleurus for introductions, talk, and some
of Alice's homemade *alcools*. Alice had been beset by a head
cold, however, and Gertrude had thought it best for the three
healthy members of the party to move outdoors. Besides,
Basket the dog needed exercise and the day was exquisite,
which Gertrude confirmed with a wide gesture of her free
hand and the pronouncement:
"Is it lovely lovelies lovely it is."
For weeks, Frank had looked forward to introducing
Carolyn to his friend Gertrude. He had thought from the
beginning that the two could become friends, though

Gertrude generally preferred the company of men. They were both smart, quick, and possessed of a natural ease here in Paris—in its marketplaces, its boulevards, its parks—that had never detracted from their other more American characteristics: their shared love of baseball, convertible automobiles, and popular cookbooks, for example. For fear that Gertrude might casually refer to the ancient suitcase conspiracy, Frank had kept the two women apart; yesterday, however, he had been reassured by news of a split in Gertrude's relationship with Ernest Hemingway. He did not know the details of the estrangement, but he had learned from Alice that Gertrude was no longer willing to discuss her past friendship with Hemingway or his increasing celebrity. With this reassurance, Frank thought it safe to introduce Gertrude to Carolyn, who had spent the morning poring over *Tender Buttons,* Gertrude's collection of prose poems, from which Carolyn had resigned ("like a defeated chess player," she said) only an hour before.

"You know, my dear," Gertrude said to Carolyn as the three strolled past the monument to Eugène Delacroix, which featured figures of Art, Time, and Glory at its base, "What I find most frustrating these days is that the public shows more curiosity about me than about my work."

"Oh?" Carolyn said. "I find your work very interesting, Miss Stein."

Frank looked at Carolyn. He knew she was little more at ease with Gertrude's highly experimental writing than he was.

"Interesting?" Gertrude asked. She mused on the word. "Michelin guidebooks are 'interesting.' My own work is probably better described as 'brilliant.'"

"Well, that word works too, of course," Carolyn said.

"You know, Alice says she has met only three geniuses in her lifetime," Gertrude continued. "And I am one."

"Oh?"

"Yes."

"Who are the others?" Carolyn asked.

"Picasso is another," Gertrude answered.

"Oh, of course. And the third?"

"Does it really matter?" Gertrude asked.

"Actually, no," Carolyn said.

"All right then."

Frank laughed. He liked Gertrude very much. She was kind and funny. And yes, brilliant.

"Frank tells me you're a writer too," Gertrude said to Carolyn.

"Oh, just magazine articles and such," she answered. "Just popular stuff."

"Nothing wrong with popular," Gertrude said.

"I guess not."

"She's very good," Frank added.

"No, nothing wrong with popular," Gertrude repeated, "Except, well, whatever's wrong with it."

"Can't argue with that," Carolyn said.

Gertrude smiled. "What's wrong with your popular writing, Carolyn?"

"Mine?"

Gertrude nodded.

"Well, if I knew how to answer that question, Miss Stein, I'd have already corrected the problem," Carolyn answered.

"Oh, come, come," Gertrude said. "We always know what's wrong with our work. We artists. Whether we admit it or not. We know better than anyone else."

Carolyn considered. "Give me an example."

"How can I? I don't know your writing."

"I mean, what's wrong with your own writing, Miss Stein?" Carolyn asked.

"Oh, my work?"

Frank held his breath.

"Well, that's a poor example," Gertrude continued. "You see, there's nothing wrong with it. But that's a very rare occurrence, you understand."

"Gertrude, Gertrude, are you this hard on everyone you meet?" Frank asked.

She shook her head. "Just friends." Then she turned back to Carolyn. "Well?"

"My writing?"

Gertrude nodded.

"Okay," Carolyn said. "I guess the writing itself is not bad, sentence by sentence. It's the subject matter that presents problems."

"And the subject matter is?"

"Fashion," Carolyn answered. "Handbags, dresses, accessories. Magazine stuff. Awful, really."

"Oh, I don't know about that," Gertrude said. "I've known some handbags, dresses, and accessories that were quite delightful. In fact, I've written a few rather heartfelt poems about them."

"'Tender buttons,'" Carolyn suggested. "Heartfelt accessories?"

Gertrude laughed. "You could say that."

"Ah, yes, Gertrude, you and fashion," Frank said, observing her drab brown corduroy skirt and vest, her sandals, and her new hair style, which was as short as a Roman emperor's.

"Don't be confused, my dear boy," she responded. "I have no need to pursue fashion. I am fashion."

Frank laughed.

"Just wait for posterity. You'll see, you foolish boy." She turned back to Carolyn. "If dresses bore you, then why do you write about them?"

"Money," Carolyn answered.

"That's a very good reason," Gertrude said. "The best, probably. But why don't you write about other things as well? On your own."

"She has," Frank said. "A novel, for example."

"Ah," Gertrude replied. "And the subject matter of your novel is not fashion, I presume?"

"The book was about a schoolgirl who gets mixed up with criminals," Carolyn said.

"I like mysteries."

"I wanted to give girls a heroine to look up to the way boys look up to their heroes," Carolyn continued. "Not just another helpless princess rescued by a knight in shining armor. I wanted my heroine to be independent and strong and intelligent. You know, like the Radio Boys or Tom Swift."

"Good idea."

Frank had read the unfinished novel, which he liked. But why wouldn't he? He found Carolyn herself on every page. For example, the heroine had been raised in the Middle West by a widowed father named Carson, the town's finest attorney and the world's finest father. She drove a blue roadster and ran a tight, very organized household. Her boyfriend held her hand but nothing more. She sat up nights with ailing spinsters and dreamed of setting the world right. "My main character was a foolish, foolish girl," Carolyn said.

Frank disagreed.

"The truth is," Carolyn continued, "all the characters came to seem foolish."

"But that's always the case," Gertrude said.

"Is it?"

"If they're based in any way upon reality," she explained, "then they'll seem fools."

"Ah, such a heroic view of humanity," Frank said.

"Don't get me wrong, dear boy. I have my heroes."

"Who are?" Frank pressed.

"As I said before, Alice has met three geniuses in her life," Gertrude answered. "They are my heroes."

"But you're one of them," Frank said.

"Yes."

"You're one of your own heroes?" he asked, smiling.

"Am I not one of your heroes?"

"Well, truthfully, yes," he said. "You are."

"See? Why should I deny myself the same inspiration?" Then she turned to Carolyn: "Now, my dear girl, tell me the real reason you abandoned your novel."

"I thought I had told you."

"No. If foolishness alone were enough to stop a writer, no book would ever be completed."

"Okay," Carolyn said. "The reason I stopped writing my book was that I learned only after starting it that the answer to important questions is never as simple as 'whodunit.'"

"Ah, the complexities of human nature," Gertrude said. "Even in a town like . . . where is your novel set?"

"River Heights."

Gertrude nodded. "I believe all writers should have two countries, the one to which they belong and the one in which they actually live."

"Is that how you do it?"

"It's not what France gives you, my dear, but what it does not take away from you that's important."

Frank was pleased—Gertrude would not have wasted

such a quotable line on a woman in whom she had no interest.

"Who is your favorite writer, Carolyn?" Gertrude asked, "Present company excluded."

"Well, I think Scott Fitzgerald is a . . . "

"Yes, yes," Gertrude interrupted. "He's very good, but let's not include writers you actually know."

"Okay. How about Anatole France?"

Gertrude nodded, approving.

"My favorite of his books used to be *The Crime of Sylvestre Bonnard*," Carolyn continued.

"Why?"

"It's about a man who raises the orphaned daughter of a woman who once broke his heart. He cares for the girl as if she's his own, though he knows she's the daughter of his rival. But jealousy doesn't matter to him. His heart is as deep as the sea. Isn't that lovely?"

"Yes. But it's not your favorite anymore?"

"Now I prefer *Revolt of the Angels*."

"You like it that the angels want to overthrow their big boss?" Gertrude asked.

"I respect their courage. And envy it."

"And whom do you wish to overthrow, Carolyn?" Gertrude asked.

Carolyn laughed as if the question held no meaning.

Frank knew better.

The three continued past the pond and stopped in a shaded quarter of the park where men sat in pairs studying chessboards.

"Let's sit," Gertrude said.

A flutist improvised somewhere nearby.

Settled, Gertrude turned to Carolyn. "I must ask you. Are your intentions toward my dear boy here honorable?"

Carolyn laughed. "No, not at all."

"Good!" Gertrude said. "'Honorable' is the last thing he needs."

"She's as disreputable as they come," Frank added. "Can't you tell just by looking at her?"

Gertrude laughed. She stood. "Watch this." She took a large handkerchief from her skirt pocket. "Let go of Basket's leash," she instructed Frank. Gertrude bent at the waist and began to wave the handkerchief at her ankle level, like a toreador waving his cape at a bull. Basket leaped for the handkerchief, which Gertrude pulled from his path; she pivoted on one sandaled foot. "Toro, toro!" she said.

Basket stopped, turned.

Gertrude bent once more, waving the handkerchief. "Come Basket. Be fierce. Play Hemingway."

The tiny dog charged once more.

Carolyn nearly fell off the bench laughing.

Frank's laughter stopped when he heard Hemingway's name.

Meantime, Gertrude executed another veronica, Basket another pass. The bullfight ended when Basket turned about once more and jumped into Gertrude's open arms.

"There, now none of us has to go to Pamplona," Gertrude said. "Ever."

"Anyone hungry?" Frank asked, anxious to change the subject from bullfighting or Spain or anything else that might introduce Hemingway into the conversation. "There's a Moroccan restaurant around the corner. Good couscous."

"*Coose-coose*, what a wonderful word," Gertrude said. "It rather amazes me that I haven't used it before in my work." She wiped her brow with the handkerchief and sat once more on the bench. "Who'd have guessed that such a fine word might have eluded me all this time?"

Frank heard nothing more. His thoughts moved suddenly away; he had noticed a woman who resembled Madame Dufour sitting on a bench near the Palais du Luxembourg. But why would the old woman be here? She did not seem the sort to holiday in the capital. Nor to holiday at all. Nonetheless, the resemblance was uncanny. And the old woman, whoever she was, seemed to be watching Frank even as he observed her.

"What is it?" Carolyn asked him.

"Excuse me for a moment, ladies," he answered. He moved up the gravel path that led toward the old woman. After a few steps he stopped.

It was she.

He stepped up his pace. By the time he reached the old woman at her bench his breath was coming fast, not from exertion, but anticipation. She looked even more worn in the sunlight than she had looked in her dimly lit house. "Madame Dufour, how glad I am to see you again."

"I've been watching you," she said. "Did you know that?"

"Yes, I saw you just now."

"I've been watching you for three days."

"Oh?"

"What kind of detective are you, Monsieur Dixon?" she asked. "Aren't detectives supposed to notice when they're being followed? Especially by an old woman who can hardly get around anymore?"

"Oh, well . . . sure," Frank said. His was neither a cautious nor a suspicious temperament, despite his profession. Of course, he needed a more satisfying explanation for Madame Dufour. "See, it's usually the detective who does the watching. That's where our energies are spent—in observation of others with little regard for our own safety."

"Oh, is that it?"

"Sure."

"You're no Sherlock Holmes."

"Well, that's true."

"But I've not been altogether disappointed with what I've observed these past few days, young man."

"Good."

"Is that young woman over there your girl?"

"Yes."

"And the other, your mother?"

"No, a friend of mine. Please, come meet them, Madame Dufour."

"I'm not here to socialize."

"All right."

She said nothing more.

"Why are you here?" Frank asked at last.

"To accept your offer."

"To find your daughter?"

The old woman nodded. "Provided, that is, that you promise never to tell me about the outcome of your investigation. Understand? You must promise to leave me in peace, whatever you learn."

"All right."

"Unless, that is, Genevieve should insist that you tell me about her whereabouts after you find her. Do you understand?"

Frank nodded.

"All right then," she said. "What you've wanted to know is this: Genevieve married an Englishman named Charles Wilson on the fifteenth of July, 1918," Madame Dufour said. "Genevieve Wilson. That's what her name would be these days, I suppose. And that's all I know."

"Oh, it's quite enough," Frank said. He stood up from the bench. "Thank you, Madame Dufour, you won't regret it. Believe me."

"I needed to be quite certain that you were not as useless as your brother," she said. "That's why I've been observing you."

"And what convinced you of my dependability?"

She nodded toward Carolyn and Gertrude across the park. "Your girl resembles Genevieve. But she is not a child, as my daughter was when your brother took her away. I like the way she carries herself. And the old woman, well, I can see that she is not one to be trifled with by anyone."

"That's true."

"Of course, I could be wrong about you," she said. "Now leave me alone."

He took her hand to kiss; she pulled it back from him before he could raise it to his lips, then she shooed him off with the same hand, as one might gesture to a troublesome child.

"Good-bye, Madame Dufour."

Frank returned to the bench where Carolyn and Gertrude waited.

"Who was that?" Carolyn asked.

"Madame Dufour. She came from Reims to see me."

"Why? Did she change her mind?"

He nodded, then smiled.

Carolyn stood, putting her hands on Frank's shoulders, emphatic in her enthusiasm. "She told you her daughter's surname?"

His smile grew wider. "It's Wilson."

"So you can find Joe's wife now?"

"I don't see why not."

"Oh Frank, this is wonderful!"

"What's this all about?" Gertrude asked.

Before Frank could speak, Carolyn volunteered an answer. "It's quite a story, Miss Stein," she began. "Let me tell you . . ."

Carolyn's recounting of Frank's private investigation washed over him like a warm breeze. He listened to her draw Gertrude into his predicament, his passion. Most marvelous, he thought, was that he did not feel a fool to hear his story told.

"Why in heaven's name have you denied me news of this investigation for so long?" Gertrude asked Frank when Carolyn finished.

"I could never have explained it to you as well as Carolyn just did," he said.

"And if Carolyn had never come along?" Gertrude asked.

"Oh, Carolyn had to come along," he answered.

"My, what a daring boy you are," Gertrude said.

Frank smiled; his daring, he thought, was just beginning.

"And there's more good news, Frank," Carolyn said.

"Oh?"

Carolyn took his hand. "I was going to tell you tonight, but now I want to share it with Miss Stein as well."

"Okay," he said, wondering how Carolyn might improve on a day already so delightful.

"Do you know Ernest Walsh?" Carolyn asked Gertrude.

"In passing," she said.

"Who is he?" Frank asked.

"He edits a literary journal called *This Quarter*, which has launched many distinguished writing careers," she answered.

Frank wondered what this had to do with him.

"Did you know that Frank is quite a good writer?" Carolyn asked Gertrude.

Frank felt his breath shorten. "What are you talking about, Carolyn?"

She smiled. "I showed Walsh those two short stories you wrote years ago."

"What?"

"I always thought they were very good," she explained.

"You did what?" Frank asked.

"I knew you'd resist, but the stories shouldn't be hidden away forever."

"Tell me you didn't, Carolyn," Frank said.

"I did, and here's the best news—he's going to publish them!"

Frank's heart sank into his stomach. "No."

Her smile broadened. "Yes, next month."

"What stories are these, my boy?" Gertrude asked.

"Unpublishable stories," he answered.

"Apparently not," Gertrude said.

"Unpublishable," he repeated. "Believe me."

"Your face has gone pale," Carolyn said to him.

"Gertrude, will you please excuse us," he said, standing.

"Of course."

"Frank, are you all right?" Carolyn asked.

"Carolyn, we have to talk."

A Midnight Walk

*She was glad there was no moon, for
the darkness afforded protection.*

Carolyn Keene
The Clue in the Diary

Carolyn Keene stood alone before the grave of her father as
the sun set behind River Heights; the city's modest skyline
was lit like a theatrical flat a few miles from the quiet cemetery. Carson Keene's funeral had occurred eight days before.
His widow, Anne, had agreed to postpone the memorial service
until later this night, which, owing to rail and steamship passage, was the earliest Carolyn could reach River Heights from
Paris. Carolyn had not yet unpacked her suitcase, which lay
in the redecorated bedroom she had occupied as a girl. Now,
standing before the grave, she felt the weight of exhaustion.
So much travel, so fast. Too fast. Not fast enough. She looked
at the headstone, which had been completed and installed
that afternoon:

CARSON KEENE
BELOVED HUSBAND AND FATHER
1875–1927

None of it seemed real.

The heart attack had occurred later the same day that Frank told her he was not the real author of the short stories she had so admired. "What fools," she said aloud. Her father, Frank, herself . . . Three individuals, one state—foolishness.

Perhaps to be alive was to be a fool, she thought.

To be dead was merely to have once been a fool and now to be, what?

Nothing?

A bank of white clouds hovered to the south. As a girl, Carolyn had pictured her mother floating in such clouds. The Reverend Barnes had described the geography of heaven as being like clouds bathed in a divine light unknown to mortals. He had further suggested a physics in heaven that was based on the absence of gravity. "Imagine the unburdening of every kind of weight and force," he suggested to the twelve-year-old girl beside the grave of her mother. Sometimes, she still thought of her mother existing in such a place. However, she could not imagine her father in similar circumstances. His was no weightless soul, whatever the Reverend Barnes might say about grace and forgiveness. Yet neither did she imagine her father consigned to a hell like the one the Reverend Barnes once described in Sunday school as being far hotter than the Sahara desert. Carolyn believed her father had suffered enough in this life for his transgressions. Now, she thought Carson Keene must be in some sort of middle place, neither Heaven nor Hell; however, she could not imagine such a place without picturing the world in which she lived now. Middle place. And as she was sure that her father was not here any longer, then where could he be?

Foolish even to ask, of course.

She never knew what her father believed about such matters. He rarely spoke to Carolyn about her mother's death or the poor woman's subsequent place in what townsfolk called the "great scheme of things." He attended church, but to Carolyn he always seemed once removed from the faith expressed by most of their neighbors. And Carolyn's own beliefs?

This brought her back to nothing.

She settled onto the soft grass beside the grave, lower, lower, until she was lying down. What would Frank say about all this? she wondered, looking into the darkening sky.

The grass was soft but cold.

On a handful of occasions over the past months Carolyn had discussed questions of God and the afterlife with Frank. He belonged to no religion, but she sometimes caught a glint of the spiritual in his eyes. He was a kind man. Most of the time kindness alone was enough of a religion, she thought. Now, she regretted whatever unkindness she had ever shown him—even the unkindness with which she had spoken after he confessed to having lied about authoring the Hemingway stories. "Damn you, Frank," she had said, pushing away from him on a sidewalk at the edge of the Luxembourg Gardens. "Damn you to hell. How could you lie to me?"

"I'm sorry."

"Why did you do it? I believed in you."

"I don't know," he said. "I was nervous that night and . . ." He searched for a word.

"And what?"

"Damn it, Carolyn, I'm a fool."

"There's no disgrace in being a fool," she said, "but that's not what you are."

He did not ask her to define what he was.

Now, she thought that "liar" was not a sufficient description of Frank Dixon, whatever notions her disappointment had inspired at the time. No one word described Frank, whom she had loved. Still loved. But he had lied to her. And what was she to do with that? How foolish can a girl be?

Hadn't her father taught her anything?

"It's over," she had told Frank.

At the time, she had thought her life could get no darker.

News of the heart attack did not reach Carolyn for three days; Anne had sent no telegram until Carson Keene's damaged heart officially ceased to beat on one of the starched hospital beds at River Heights Memorial. Anne explained in her correspondence that she had not wanted to wire "unnecessary worry" and that there had been nothing Carolyn could do anyway, "so far away from your father's poor failing heart in the first place." Carolyn threw her clothes into a trunk, cashed out her account at the Crédit Lyonnaise, secured transportation, resigned from *Vogue* magazine, and scribbled notes to half a dozen friends to explain her misfortune and sudden departure from Paris. Frank rode the train with her to Calais. By then, however, the two were barely speaking. Still, it was only with difficulty that she resisted his offer to accompany her all the way back to River Heights. She boarded the White Star steamer that would take her across the Channel to Dover, where she would travel further by rail to Southampton and then on to the *Mauretania* for the Atlantic crossing, a journey more somber than the passage she had undertaken years before with Count Orlovsky and the

Fitzgeralds. She did not stand on the deck among the other voyagers to wave good-bye to Frank.

She still loved him.

But she would not be lied to.

Now, she sat up on the grass beside the freshly turned dirt of her father's grave. Beloved husband and father. She did not want to be angry at Carson Keene. She wanted to be forgiving, her mind open to the frailties of human nature, her heart filled only by loving memories of this man who had made of her girlhood a shining period. Nonetheless, she could not help but wonder to whom the words carved in stone ("beloved husband and father") were intended to refer? When Anne paid the stonecutter for the slab that was set now in the soft soil, she had surely considered herself his only loving wife. Carolyn's mother, buried with her own parents on the other side of the cemetery, was no part of those who had loved Carson as husband—at least as far as the stone for which Anne's bank check had paid was concerned. Just as surely, Carolyn suspected, Anne considered little Rose to be the sole loving subject of his fatherhood. Of course, Anne would never admit such a thing to Carolyn, whom she had embraced an hour before at the train station with sorrowful eyes and a warm, consoling smile.

But Carolyn did not want to indulge thoughts like these.

Instead, she chose to recall the time fifteen years before when the police had picked her up walking along the road, two days and two cold nights into the first leg of her planned journey around the globe. She recalled the police wagon pulling into the driveway of the Keene home and Carolyn's mother running off the porch, tears streaming down her face. She took Carolyn into her arms, rocking her. "My baby, my baby," she said. "I've been so worried." When she let go, Carolyn saw her father kneeling beside her. His eyes too were weary; however, he did not coddle Carolyn but shared with her what she thought of as a conspiratorial smile, as if he had known all along that she would be safe wherever she might go—not because the world was safe but because Carolyn was so capable. She smiled back to him. Then he winked at her, and Carolyn rejoiced that her father seemed to understand without explanation her reasons for undertaking the journey. So what if she was only nine years old? He believed in her.

She had believed in him.

Perhaps he was not a bad man, she thought, opening her eyes.

But when had she closed her eyes?

She sat up, coming full awake now on the cold grass. Darkness lay all about her. When had she fallen asleep? How long had she been sleeping? She looked at her wristwatch. "Good God," she muttered. Hours had passed. It was nine o'clock. She jumped to her feet.

The memorial service had begun at seven. She had missed it.

After a moment of panic, she discovered herself relieved. "I don't need you, River Heights, any more than you need me," she said aloud.

She started for her father's house.

By the time she arrived, the place was crowded with cocktail-wielding mourners.

"Carolyn!" they all called. "Carolyn, Carolyn, we were so worried about you! Are you all right? Poor girl. You look . . . tired. Where've you been? It's me, your old friend George. Don't you recognize me, dear? What in heaven's name are you wearing? It's me, Ned, Ned Nickerson. Come and meet my wife. And the kids. We all want to express our sympathies. He was a great man, Carolyn. But you know that better than anyone. Are you all right? Come, have a drink. It's me—Bess. You don't recognize me, Carolyn, do you? It's because I've lost so much weight. We're so sorry about your father, but the service was beautiful. What a shame you missed it. Reverend Barnes himself broke down. You should have seen it, Carolyn. You'd have been so proud."

Then Anne pushed through the crowd that had gathered about Carolyn. "How on earth could you have missed your own father's service?"

Carolyn tried to speak, but no words came.

"We waited all these days just so you could be here," Anne continued. "If you didn't care to come we could have done the whole thing all at once, like it's supposed to be done."

"I have to go and clean up," Carolyn said. "My clothes are dirty. And they're all wrong, I know. They're for traveling. Not for this. Excuse me, please."

Carolyn felt all of their eyes on her as she climbed the stairs to her old room.

There she closed and locked the door behind her. She washed her face, applied lipstick and eyeliner, powder and rouge, and changed into a clean dress. Then she crept down the back stairway, through the pantry, and into the basement, which she could still navigate in the dark; she climbed up the creaky ladder that led to the storm doors, which she unlocked and pushed open. Then she stepped up and out of the darkness and into the moonlit garden, where once her mother had grown a patch of sweet peas; Carolyn had been allowed to pick whole bunches on special occasions. The house glowed from within. Townsfolk moved past the windows with drinks in their hands. A cocktail party worthy of Carson Keene, Carolyn thought. She hoped no one saw her in the yard. She moved toward the trees, beyond which lay the rest of the world. She did not know where to go.

She stopped in the shadows of the trees.

Here, she should be safe from eyes, she thought.

But here, crouched in the shadows, she suddenly felt watched.

"Who's there?" she called, turning about.

No one.

She passed through the trees to the deserted gravel road; she started up the shoulder and away from the house. Sometimes as she walked she thought she heard other footsteps, but each time she turned back she saw only the empty road. Perhaps the sound came from the bushes, she thought. Birds settling for the night into their nests, probably. No matter. All was still when she came to a junction. No cars in any direction. No electric lights. Nonetheless, this was a center of the world, she realized, moving to the center of the gravel intersection. The axis of an X—like the precise spot where the Boulevard St-Germain and the Boulevard St-Michel cross, or the spot where Broadway crosses 42nd Street in Manhattan, or the intersection of State Street and Madison in Chicago, or Oxford Street and Charing Cross Road in London. This spot, where she stood now, was as central as any other on the true map of the universe, even if at this moment no one could know that she occupied the axis of this central X. She breathed deeply here. But she could not stand at the center of the crossroads all night long (or all her life), however much she might like to.

She moved on.

The River Heights Elementary School, another quarter mile down the road, looked much the same as Carolyn remembered its having looked the first time she saw it, which had been more than twenty years before. She had been five years old. The night was dark, like tonight. But it could not have been late. In those days, Carolyn's bedtime had been eight-thirty. Now, she crossed the road, pushed the wooden gate open, and stepped onto the school grounds. In 1907, her father had brought her here so she would feel familiar with the environs the next day, which was to be her first as a kindergartner. He had held her hand as they walked for the first time into the schoolyard; for a long time he had sat beside her on a swing that hung from the thick limb of an oak.

Now the schoolyard was empty. Silent.

"For you, Carolyn, kindergarten is going to be a breeze," he had told her as they sat together on the swing. Then he had pressed gently backwards, lifting the swing into the air to the height of his long, long legs. "Hold on to the ropes," he said. Then he lifted his feet from the ground and they slid forward through the night air in a smooth arc. "Feel it?" he asked. "The breeze."

Yes, she had felt the breeze on her face.

"That's kindergarten," he said as they swung backwards in the same arc. "Nothing to it."

Now, a swing hung from the same branch. Carolyn wondered if the smooth, three-foot-long slab of wood was the same that had once borne the weight of her father and herself. Surely the ropes by which the swing was suspended had been changed many times in the years since. She pushed the swing into an arc. It sliced the air. Back and forth—finally settling once more to stillness. Then she looked up at the oak; it looked the same as she remembered, though the tree must have grown substantially in the years since Carolyn had last been here. She wondered if it looked the same to her because she and the tree had, over the years, grown in the same proportion to one another. She turned toward the five buildings that comprised the school. Unlike the tree, they had not grown to keep pace with her. Once, these school grounds had seemed to Carolyn as big and complex as a city.

Then a sound.

"Is someone there?" she asked, turning back toward the tree.

No one.

Then a girl's laughter from the shadows near the auditorium.

Carolyn turned toward the sound. "Who's there?"

"Just me." A girl child stepped forward. Her face remained in the shadows. "I followed you."

"Who are you?"

"Why would you come to school when you don't have to?" the girl asked. "Are you crazy or something?"

"A little crazy."

"I should say so. Coming to school when you don't have to."

"Don't you like school?" Carolyn asked.

"When you were a girl, did you?"

"As a matter of fact I did."

"Yeah, you're crazy all right."

"Who are you?" Carolyn repeated.

The girl stepped into the moonlight. "It's me. Rose."

The breath caught in Carolyn's throat. Rose. Anne's daughter. And her father's daughter. "Oh, well," Carolyn said. She was surprised at how small a five-year-old looks in the moonlight. "It's nice to meet you," she managed. "I've been looking forward to it for some time."

"Me too," Rose said.

"But what are you doing out here?"

"I told you, I followed you."

"But it's late, Rose. You shouldn't be outdoors. It's cold. And dark. You should be home."

"You're not my mother, you know," Rose answered. "You're my sister. So there."

Sister, Carolyn thought.

"Besides, I'm not the only one being bad right now," Rose continued. "You're being bad too. We're both being bad."

"Are we?" Carolyn asked.

"Yes, but you're bad most of the time, aren't you?"

"What?"

"Oh, it's all right," Rose said. "I'm quite bad too. I don't think I'd like you much if you were any other way."

"What makes you think you like me?"

"I've been watching you."

"And?"

"You're as bad as they say. I like that."

"Who says I'm bad?"

"I can't tell you."

"My father never said it, did he?"

"You mean, our father?"

"Oh, yes."

"No, he never said anything about you being bad," Rose said. "But that's all right. I liked you anyway, even if he was always telling me how good you were when you were a girl. And how I should be more like you. I always knew he was lying."

Lying, Carolyn thought.

"I knew you were no goody-two-shoes," Rose continued. "Whatever Dad said. Or the grocer who told me you'd have never tried to sneak a handful of his candy bars out of his store hidden in the pocket of your dress."

"Did you do that?"

"So what if I did?"

"Naughty."

"Oh, don't bother," Rose said. "I've always been onto you. And then when Mother called you 'wicked,' well . . ."

"Well what?"

Rose smiled. "Then I knew we were really sisters."

Carolyn moved toward the girl, who was as pretty as her pictures. Her smile was warm. Her eyes were bright. "I doubt that you're as wicked as all that," Carolyn said. She had not expected to feel such affection for this girl. She held her hand out. "It's nice to meet you Rose."

Rose shook her hand. "I followed you from the moment you climbed out of the basement."

"You're very stealthy."

"Very what?"

"Stealthy," Carolyn said. "Like an Indian. Clever and quiet."

"Oh, yes, that's true. I am."

"Why did you follow me?"

"Because I wanted to meet you, of course."

"That's nice. But don't you think your mother will worry?"

"No. She's busy tonight. We can do whatever we want, you and me."

"Oh."

"Why did you come here alone?"

"Tonight?" Carolyn asked.

"I mean here. River Heights. Don't you have a husband?"

"No," she said.

"Why not?"

"Not everybody has a husband."

"Men don't," Rose said. "They have wives."

"Not all people are married."

"You mean old maids?"

"No, not just 'old maids,'" Carolyn said. "Some people don't want to marry."

"Don't you?"

"Well sure, someday."

"But not now?"

Carolyn shrugged. "How about you, Rose?"

"Me, get married?" The girl smiled. "Well, actually, I do want to get married. As soon as possible."

"Soon?"

"Bobby Crandall. He's very bad. Like us. And he's very cute."

"Bad and cute," Carolyn mused.

Rose's smile widened.

"Watch out for that kind," Carolyn suggested.

"Why did you come here?" Rose asked. "To school, I mean. You didn't really like school when you were a girl, did you?"

Carolyn shrugged.

"Do you want to throw a rock through a window?" Rose asked.

"What?"

"We could break some of the glass."

"Rose! You don't really do that kind of thing, do you?"

"Never yet, but now that you're here . . ."

"No."

"Well, Dad's not here anymore," Rose said. "So why shouldn't we do whatever we want?"

"No, Rose, it's not like that."

"We'll never be good again, okay? Ever! Why should we?"

"He wouldn't want us to be like that."

"Who cares what he wants," Rose said. "He's dead, Carolyn. Didn't you know that? He went and died. That's what he did. Haven't they told you what that means? He's gone forever. Never coming back. He didn't care what we wanted, so why should we care about what he wants?"

"Oh, he cared about us."

"Then why did he go and die?"

"He couldn't help it."

"That's no excuse."

"Yes, it is," Carolyn said.

"Mother says 'I can't help it' is never an acceptable excuse."

"Well, 'never' is a pretty powerful word. Maybe too powerful."

"So what's a better word?"

"'Sometimes,'" Carolyn answered.

"'Sometimes' is better than 'never'?"

"Always," Carolyn said.

"What?"

"Well, almost always . . ."

"What are you talking about, Carolyn?" Rose asked.

Carolyn laughed, despite herself. "I don't know."

"Okay."

"But I know that he cared about us," Carolyn continued. "And you know that too, don't you?"

"Maybe."

"Sure."

"Then I'll tell you who's to blame," Rose said.

"Nobody's to blame."

"My mother killed him," Rose said.

"What? No."

"It's true."

"Why do you say that?"

"Because his heart stopped working."

"Yes, so?"

"You know what I used to hear him say to my mother, almost every night?"

Carolyn shook her head.

"'You're breaking my heart, Anne. Breaking my heart.' That's what he used to say. And then, I guess, she did. For good."

"No, Rose. He didn't mean it like that."

"Then how did he mean it?"

Suddenly, Carolyn had no words. "Well, it's not like you think it is. Your mother didn't kill him. He just . . . died."

Tears started suddenly from Rose's eyes.

Carolyn dropped to her knees and opened her arms to the girl, who fell into them.

"I'm not crying," Rose said.

"I know."

"I'm afraid," Rose said.

"Of being without your dad?"

"Our dad," she corrected.

"Our dad," Carolyn said.

"No, I'm afraid of going to school."

"Kindergarten?"

Rose nodded.

Carolyn pulled the girl closer. "Don't be afraid, Rose. Kindergarten's a breeze."

Rose looked at Carolyn. "That's what he said."

"I know."

"He couldn't help it?" Rose asked.

"Dad?"

The girl nodded. "Dying."

"That's right," Carolyn said. "He couldn't help it. None of it."

"And that's an excuse?"

"Yes."

"Always?"

"Sometimes," Carolyn answered.

"This time?"

"Yes."

"But not all the time?"

Carolyn thought of Frank. "No," she said. "Not all the time."

"Why are you crying, Carolyn?" Rose asked.

Carolyn wiped her cheeks. "I miss him."

"Dad?"

"Yes. Dad and . . ." She stopped.

"Who?"

"Nobody," she said.

"Who's 'nobody'?"

Carolyn shook her head. "Don't worry, Rose. It's all right. It has to be. Because there's nothing to be done. Do you understand?"

"Not really."

"That's okay. I don't really understand either."

"Is that why you came here?" Rose asked. "To the school, I mean. To learn?"

Carolyn shook her head. "I'm too old for that."

"Too bad."

"Yes."

In a London Fog

Lupin walked as one walks in a dream,
one of those queer dreams in which the
most inconsequent things occur.

Maurice Leblanc
The Confessions of Arsène Lupin

The rain had ceased these past two weeks only long enough for a gritty, brown fog to settle from time to time over the streets of London, where Frank had taken a room in the same hotel on Russell Square that he had first occupied six years before.

Now it was teatime. Frank sipped Earl Grey from a china cup.

He did not much like tea.

The lobby was quiet but for the tinkling of spoons and the half-whispered conversations of other guests who were all dressed more elegantly than Frank. In Paris, he had packed haphazardly, tossing shirts, socks, and undergarments into a pile on his bed before closing and locking his battered suitcase about them. A man's mind can contain only so much at any one moment, he reflected. In those hours he had been occupied by the more urgent prospect of catching a cab to the Gare du Nord, where he was to meet Carolyn and accompany her as far as she would allow on her trip back to America. He hoped she would let him stay with her the whole way. He knew how she suffered at the news of her father's death; he ached for her, even as he ached himself over the chill that had come over their relationship since he confessed to lying about the Hemingway stories. When he met her at the train station, he would find in her eyes the answer to the question of whether they might yet be together. What then could packing clothes matter to him on such a night? What did it matter now? Wrinkles in his trousers. So what?

Teatime, goddamnit. So he sipped again.

He had not felt this way the first time he stayed at this hotel. Six years is a long time, he thought. However, most of the reversals that swamped Frank now had occurred in the last two weeks—that is, since Carolyn had departed Calais without him. He had watched her ship recede from the harbor. Afterward, he went into the ferry offices and bought himself a ticket for Dover—not to pursue Carolyn (though his initial impulse had been to do just that), but to undertake an exploration of the Public Records building on Whitehall Street where British census records were stored and where he might discover a record of his brother's wife, Genevieve Wilson. Carolyn might steam away, he thought, but that need not deter him from his life's work. Even so, on the train ride up from Dover, and on numerous occasions during his first days in London, he had discovered himself wondering where Carolyn was on her voyage. In this manner, he plotted in his mind her course across the Atlantic, even as he undertook his investigation of the interior of the massive British records building, which was occupied by files shelved in aisles almost as dusty and twisting as the catacombs of Paris. He was glad for the nearly incomprehensible filing system— he needed all the distraction he could find. Millions of sheets of yellowing paper: the roll call of the British Empire. Another abandoned lover might have drowned his sorrows in Scotch whiskey or stout British ale while in England. For Frank, work always served better than drinking to distract him from his ills. Not the private detective work he did about the Left Bank for money. But his real work.

Joe, Genevieve.

His exploration of the subterranean British records office was not without result. What he found, however, offered no relief.

Genevieve was dead. The ill-typed records were concise but sufficient—an entry visa, a death certificate. Mere facts: Genevieve Wilson (née Dufour, Dixon) native of Reims, France, wife of Charles Wilson of Swaffham, England, had died of influenza in the town of Dover in January 1919.

Frank sought an obituary in the public library.

No luck.

Only Madame Dufour would understand the loss, he thought. But Frank could not contact the old woman. Not ever. He had given her his word.

Which seemed to leave nothing to be done.

Still, Frank had not left London.

Where was he to go?

He feared Paris would never again seem like a home. But neither could he return to America knowing that Carolyn was there too, close enough that he might reach her by train only to find her resolved still to be apart from him (as she had suggested in a letter that arrived a few days before from River Heights). No, he needed an ocean between himself and further heartbreak, he thought. And yet he could not remain at the Russell Hotel either. His money would run out soon.

And the rain was oppressive.

By evening, Frank was once again meandering the streets.

He stopped outside the British Museum on Great Russell Street where a crowd was gathering.

A lecture.

Anything to pass an hour or two, he thought.

Inside, the audience settled and then applauded as a small man from the museum introduced the evening's speaker.

"Ladies and gentlemen, it is my pleasure to welcome to the podium tonight the distinguished author and world-renowned psychic researcher, Sir Arthur Conan Doyle."

Frank sat up, suddenly attentive.

He had attended a lecture of Conan Doyle's once before, in New York City. Conan Doyle was famous for creating Sherlock Holmes; however, the subject of the lecture in America had not been the fictional detective, but spiritualism. Frank had been moved by Conan Doyle's presentation; his "spirit photographs," projected as slides on a large screen in the lecture hall, created a palpable sense of yearning among the audience; the sincerity of his explanations of the working of ectoplasm and other technical aspects of life after death, combined with the almost magical workings of darkness in the lecture hall, made it impossible not to be moved. Of course, foolishness. . . . But even now Frank thought it strange that of all lecturers to have stumbled across he should discover himself here, applauding with others for Conan Doyle, who made his way across the stage toward the podium with the lumbering power of a bear.

"People ask me, not unnaturally, what it is that makes me so perfectly certain that this thing called spiritualism is true," Conan Doyle began.

For the next hour and twenty minutes, the old man attempted to explain his convictions. First, he recalled séances wherein the medium had revealed to Conan Doyle details of personal relationships that only a departed friend or relative could know; next, the lights were dimmed, and three mediums who had taken chairs on the stage went into trances to deliver personal messages from spirits they claimed were hovering about the room; finally, after an emotional equilibrium was regained by those to whom the spirit messages had been addressed (which did not include Frank), Conan Doyle moved on to a display of spirit photographs, many of which Frank recognized from the first lecture in New York City.

Then Conan Doyle took questions.

Do spirits always tell the truth to mediums?

In the spirit realm, do our loved ones always inhabit bodies comparable to the ones they left behind on earth?

Do spirits experience conflict with one another on the astral plane?

Conan Doyle answered the questions with confidence.

Then a young woman stood. She looked lovely and grave in the auditorium's light. "What can one do to increase the chances that a departed spirit might contact a bereaved relation?" she asked.

"You mean a spirit that has otherwise demonstrated re-luctance for contact?" Conan Doyle responded.

"Yes, reluctance," she said.

Frank noticed a tear on the woman's cheek.

"Well, my dear," Conan Doyle answered, "the best thing you can do is to bring to your next séance a relic or souvenir of the spirit's earthly life. This demonstrates to the spirit your continued interest in him. Of course, you must choose the relic carefully."

Without thinking Frank stood. "And if the spirit refuses contact, even after one offers up a well-chosen relic or souvenir?" he asked.

Conan Doyle nodded, his expression sympathetic. "Then hold tight, young man, to whatever object you chose to bring to the séance, even if the spirit does not contact you. After all, a spirit's shadow is often cast upon such objects."

Frank's impulse was to offer doubting words to the old man. But the impulse passed quickly.

He nodded, then sat.

Relics, souvenirs. Well, perhaps.

The next day Frank hired a car.

Charles Wilson resided at 22 White Birch Road in Swaffham, a rural market town an hour-and-a-half drive east of London. Frank did not know if Wilson would talk to him. The Englishman had ignored Frank's correspondence. Frank did not blame him. Nonetheless, Frank needed to know if Genevieve had possessed some relic or souvenir of her time with Joe that had survived not only Joe's disappearance, but also Genevieve's subsequent marriage to Wilson, and her own death, to lie unclaimed these years in some dusty drawer in the house at 22 White Birch Road. A marriage photo, a locket, a letter. Anything of Joe from his period in France was better than nothing, Frank thought.

He had no trouble finding the Wilson residence, which was not far from the center of town. The house was modest and neat.

He knocked on the door.

The door opened.

Frank's breath caught in his chest. The man before him was not Charles Wilson.

It was his brother.

"Joe?" Frank said.

No answer.

Frank recalled Conan Doyle's photographic slides of spirits; he turned and looked for a witness (a postman, a milkmaid, a farmer, any passer-by) to confirm that the man standing before him was actually there. But the street was deserted. He turned back. Cautiously, he extended his fingertips to touch Joe's face.

"Hello, Frank," Joe said. "I suspected that one day you'd find me."

Frank stepped back. "My God, it's you."

Joe nodded.

"Joe!" Frank grabbed his brother and pulled him close. "Do you know how long I've been looking for you?"

Joe returned the embrace. "Come inside," he said.

But now Frank could not move. "Joe, I'm here as your brother, not as some kind of investigator. Do you understand?" He did not wait for an answer. Rather, words spilled from Frank in a torrent, flooding from his heart and bypassing his overworked brain altogether. "I don't need to know what happened all those years ago in France, Joe. Not if you don't want to talk about it. Once, I thought I needed to know. Five minutes ago I thought I needed to know. But now I'm just happy to see you. Do you understand that?"

"We've got some catching up to do," Joe said. "You got a little time?"

"I've got nothing but time." He meant it literally.

"Come inside."

Frank followed his brother into the house. Joe's house? he wondered. His head swam. After all these years, he discovered himself still unprepared for this most anticipated moment. "Joe's house," he whispered to himself, as if speaking the words aloud could make the notion seem less unreal. "Joe Dixon, Joe Dixon . . ." he whispered.

"What'd you say?" Joe asked, turning to Frank.

"Oh, nothing."

Joe raised the blinds, flooding the room with light. Frank looked at him. He was worn and thin, his eyes set deeply in his head. He had been aged by more than just the years that had passed, Frank thought.

"Welcome to my home," Joe said.

"How long have you lived here?"

"Years now."

"So, who's Charles Wilson?" Frank asked.

"He's me," Joe answered.

"A pseudonym?"

"A *nom de guerre.*"

"But the war is over," Frank said.

"More over for some than others."

Frank said nothing.

"What do you think of the place?" Joe asked, indicating with a sweep of his hand the room in which they stood.

"Very nice," Frank said. The room was sparsely furnished. A worn sofa was set before a stone fireplace; a low bookshelf ran half the length of one wall; a pair of straight-backed chairs were arranged around a tea table upon which stood a bottle of rye. A battered desk beside the window was piled with papers and topped on one shelf by two framed photographs: one, a picture of Genevieve (whom Frank recognized from the album Madame Dufour had shown him in Reims); the other, a photo of a boy about eight years old in school uniform with cap and tie. "And who's this?" Frank asked, pointing to the boy's photograph.

"That's Charles Wilson's son."

"What are you saying, Joe?"

"That's my son."

Frank sat on the sofa, his head and heart suddenly too full for his legs to bear standing. "You're a father?"

Joe nodded.

"Where is he?"

"He's away at school."

"What's his name?"

"François," Joe said. "But I call him Frank."

Frank stood once more. Years of yearning and uncertainty welled inside him. And anger too, which he had not expected. How had Joe denied him this? A nephew! Why? He crossed the room to the photograph. "He's a beautiful boy."

Joe nodded.

"And Genevieve is his mother?"

"Yes."

"But she died?"

"Yes," Joe said, moving across the room. "I need a drink. Do you want one?"

"Not now."

Joe went to the bottle of rye. He poured two glasses, then handed one to Frank. "Take it anyway."

Frank took the glass and drank it at a gulp. He hadn't known he was so dry. "Give me another."

Joe obliged.

Frank drank it again at a gulp.

"I owe you an apology," Joe said.

Frank said nothing.

"For disappearing," Joe continued.

Frank shook his head. "Not for disappearing," he said. "But for staying disappeared all this time."

Joe nodded.

"Why?" Frank asked. "I don't understand."

"I thought you said you hadn't come here as an investigator."

"That's before I knew I was an uncle," Frank answered.

Joe said nothing.

"Put down your drink," Frank said.

Joe put his glass on an end table.

"Put up your fists," Frank continued.

"What?"

"Your fists," Frank said.

Joe did nothing.

Frank punched Joe on the point of the chin, knocking him over a chair and onto a rug near the front door.

After a moment, Joe sat up.

"I told you to put up your fists," Frank said.

"Yeah, thanks for the warning."

"Sorry. I shouldn't have punched you in your own house."

"I deserved it," Joe answered from the floor as he rubbed his chin. "Actually, I deserve much worse."

"How old is your boy?"

"Eight."

"Ah, Joe." Frank went to his brother. He offered him a hand up.

"You pack a pretty good punch these days," Joe said.

Frank looked at his brother. Joe Dixon, here before him now—alive, safe. But not the same.

The old Joe would never have left his guard down.

"You all right, Frank? You look like you're the one who's just been punched."

"Do you remember the last day we spent together in Bayport, Joe?"

Joe shook his head.

"We'd ridden our motorcycles to the Point, overlooking town," Frank reminded him.

"Oh, yeah."

"There's something I've wished for years I'd said to you that day."

"What?"

"I wish I'd told you not to go to France," Frank said. "Damn, you were just a kid. I was old enough to know that war was no lark."

"Frank, it wasn't your place to 'tell' me what to do."

"I know. What I mean is, I wish I'd asked you not to go."

"You did ask me not to go, Frank."

"Did I?"

Joe nodded.

Frank could not speak. Rather, he began to laugh, though none of what was happening was funny.

Joe stepped back, confused.

Frank laughed harder and harder until at last his laughter turned to tears. "Joe, all these years?"

"Yeah," Joe said, his expression far away.

"Why?"

"It's a long story."

"I told you, I've got nothing but time."

"Sit down, Frank."

Many hours later, long after midnight—alone in a spare bedroom in Joe's house—Frank began writing a letter to his mother and father that he would never send. A portion follows:

> . . . and he spent many nights surreptitiously away
> from his barracks. Of course, Joe knew he could face
> court martial if he was ever caught. But he said he
> could no longer muster the courage to climb into his

airplane without slipping away some nights to be with his wife, Genevieve, who had become his reason for carrying on.

It was on one such night that his barracks were hit by enemy fire, turning his sleeping comrades to ash. Joe arrived, unsuspecting, the next morning on a bicycle borrowed from a local friend. He stumbled among the wrecked buildings and terrible carnage. The fire crews did not recognize him. He was dazed and heartbroken by the loss. He started across the airfield toward headquarters, intending to report to duty, when he realized that by military rationale he had been guilty of desertion under fire, an offense punishable by execution.

Of course, there was nothing he might have accomplished by being asleep among his comrades. Except to die along with them. But military tribunals were not merciful in those war-mad days. Joe swears he'd have continued to headquarters anyway, facing whatever sentence a tribunal passed, had it not been that he had learned only days before that his wife was pregnant.

Yes, Mother and Dad, more on that later . . .

So, rather than report for court martial, Joe slipped away from the airfield and returned with Genevieve to Paris where he secured a false identity. Charles Wilson, Englishman. Mr. and Mrs. Wilson traveled to Dover shortly before the Armistice. There, Genevieve bore their child. Within weeks, however, she was struck down by flu. Joe and his infant son moved to Swaffham, where they have lived ever since.

I made Joe understand our anguish at his disappearance. But Joe had his reasons, I suppose.

At first he feared that any correspondence to us would be intercepted by authorities who could still arrest him for desertion. Time passed and Joe eventually came to feel safe from military prosecution; by then, however, he had learned that a memorial service was held for him in Bayport. Naturally, he assumed we thought he'd died; at that point he chose not to alter our misconception, preferring that we think of him as a dead hero rather than a living deserter. I assured him he was wrong. Nonetheless, shame registers on his expression like a permanent shadow. When I first saw him I thought I'd encountered a ghost. You can imagine my joy when I discovered otherwise. But now, after spending most of the day and all of one night with him, I realize that in some ways he is indeed a ghost. He has been sad for so long, Mother and Dad. Sad at having lost his wife. Sad at having lost his self-respect. But, of course, he is alive and so hope remains. And he loves his boy, though he has sent him far away to school because he seems to fear being known too well by anyone—even his own family, perhaps particularly his own family.

My arrival has not been easy for Joe. Last week I sent a letter of inquiry to the man I believed was Charles Wilson, and so Joe was not surprised to see me at his doorstep. Yet, I cannot reassure him enough of my understanding to make him comfortable with me—or rather, with himself. But then it's only been one day. Maybe tomorrow or the day after, he'll grow more at ease. Naturally, I want to meet his son. But Joe remains reluctant. I assured him I would betray no secrets, respecting the life he has made with his boy, whatever the guidelines. I even suggested he could introduce me as a friend, a cousin, or however he wants.

Joe sleeps now in his bedroom, separated from the room in which I write this letter by one thin wall and nine long years. I hope he is sleeping well. I fear he is not. But we are together again. Doesn't that suggest that anything is possible? Truly, anything . . .

Frank set the letter down beside his bed and settled onto the soft mattress. It would be light outside in a few hours. He closed his eyes. His head swam. So much had changed, so fast. Perhaps he would stay in England to be near Joe and his boy, he thought. He could open a detective agency in London. Or perhaps his brother could be persuaded to move with his son to Paris, where Frank's competence in the business of recovering *les disparus* could require no greater testimonial than the mere presence of Joe Dixon, recovered from what had seemed oblivion. He imagined sitting beside the Thames or the Seine telling his nephew stories of the adventurous boyhoods Joe and he had shared in Bayport.

Why not?

Except that Joe had changed since Frank last shared adventures with him.

In the morning, Frank awoke alone in the house.

He moved from room to room. Sometime in the night, pictures had been removed from the walls. The closet in Joe's room was empty of clothes. The boy's bedroom had been cleaned out of everything but furniture. Frank went to the front door and stepped outside. The car that had been parked on the pebbled driveway was gone.

"Joe!" he called.

No answer.

Later, Frank discovered a note from Joe scrawled on the back of the unfinished letter Frank had left beside his bed the night before.

How had Joe been so stealthy?

Frank wondered again if he had spent the previous day in the company of a ghost.

But the note was real.

Frank—

I love you as a brother, but I'm not Joe Dixon any- more. Not ever again. Don't you know that Joe Dixon was a deserter, regardless of extenuating circum- stances? Deserter. Look, it's better if you just imagine that he died in the fire that consumed his comrades.

Try to understand—it's not that I can't face up to you and Mother and Dad. It's that I can't tell my son that his life has been a lie. He must never know the truth about me. Years ago I made a choice. Perhaps it was mistaken, but I am committed to it. I am Charles Wilson.

You were always the smart one. I might have beaten you in an arm wrestle or a footrace, but I could never outthink you. You're still the smart one. I'm sure you could find me again if you put your mind to it. England is not that big. But please don't look for me. You mentioned last night that you'd fallen in love with a girl in Paris but that you'd lost her. Well, get her back, Frank. Do it for yourself—you deserve only the best.

And then carry on, relieved of your terrible responsibilities.

Affectionately,
Charles Wilson

Chapter the Last

*It is only ourselves that we
find in books.*

Anatole France
The Red Lily

Alone, Carolyn Keene paced the small living room of her old friend Bess Marvin's apartment on Ninth Street in Greenwich Village. Bess had arrived here from River Heights two years before, inspired to change her life, in part, by the postcards Carolyn had sent her from abroad.

Now it was late afternoon.

Carolyn had moved in with Bess shortly after Carson Keene's memorial service, almost three months before. In that time, she had done a lot of pacing about this room, sometimes in anticipation of one or another of the diversions that Bess and her bohemian friends provided, at other times merely to dispel the energies (fear, anger, regret) that built inside her, like a penance for her sins. An hour of pacing was better than a pint of bootleg whiskey, she had discovered. Better too than the reefer that Bess brought home from time to time. Carolyn did not know for sure what her sins had been, but she had some ideas: perhaps that her father had died without whatever solace might have been provided by her forgiveness, which she had discovered aching within her like a sickened internal organ only after he was gone; perhaps that she had left her little sister back in River Heights, despite the affection she felt for the girl, because Carolyn had neither the resources nor the technical grounds to take the child from her mother; perhaps that she had merely shaken Frank Dixon's hand when they parted in France instead of pressing her lips to his and whispering that she loved him still, even if she could not forgive him for his misrepresentation, a characteristic more damning of herself, she knew, than of Frank.

When had all this happened to the Carolyn Keene who at seventeen had seemed so well equipped for the world?

But things were changing, she hoped.

Today. This hour.

She turned to the picture window near the sofa, parting the curtains and looking three flights down to the neighborhood. No sign of Bess yet. She settled onto the window seat and watched the crowds below move about the sidewalks and street corners. Like her, many among them had returned from abroad these past months.

Expatriates, returned.

She let the curtain fall closed. She resumed pacing.

"Ex-expatriates," she said aloud.

For the past six weeks, Carolyn had worked at her old job at the Proper Pagan Tea Room; in that time, Bess had attempted to secure an editorial position for her at G. & D. Publishers, where Bess had been working for almost two years as an illustrator of children's books. Nothing had opened up. Carolyn did not mind. She had come to New

York with no specific ambitions, except to get away from River Heights (accomplished), reconnect with her friend Bess (accomplished), and rediscover something of her sense of emotional balance (not yet accomplished). The waitress job had suited her well. She had enjoyed the moment-by-moment nature of the work, delivering tea and coffee to strangers who thanked her, paid her, and then went away. Sometimes repeat customers offered gestures of familiarity—nods that acknowledged having shared with Carolyn the same smoky air for an hour or two in the heavily draped room; or sometimes they shared a word about the weather or a light-hearted sentence about tea and biscuits or an unsolicited appraisal of President Coolidge's latest policy decision. From time to time, a young man asked Carolyn to leave the tea room for an afternoon walk around Washington Square or an evening at a theater or jazz club or some other place where she might be his guest rather than his waitress. She bore these suitors no ill will, but she did not accept their offers either.

That is, until Harold Burke walked into the tea room.

Here in New York they had met years before.

Harold: old enough to be her father, accomplished artist, literary critic, and publisher. Womanizing rat, as well. Years before, Carolyn had discovered only after their romantic affair was full blown that he was a married man. There and then, she had sworn never to see him again.

But that was years ago. Now he was divorced.

True, since leaving New York in 1923 she had not once missed him.

Also true, however, was that she felt more alone now than ever.

She glanced at her wristwatch. Almost four. She had set her suitcase beside the door. What could be keeping Bess, she wondered, who was already twenty minutes late. Carolyn did not want to be alone when Harold arrived, which could be any moment now. And worse, if Bess were not back by 4:15, then Carolyn would have to leave the apartment alone with Harold. Silly, she thought. What sense did it make that Carolyn wanted Bess's company to Grand Central Station when from that point forward she would be alone with Harold all the way to Boston anyway?

No sense.

A month before, Carolyn had written a long letter to Frank. In it, she had apologized for the angry manner of her departure. Her letter did not go so far as to absolve him; she was still wary of loving a man who was unable to make good on his claims (though she did not doubt the goodness of his heart). Still, she no longer wanted silence between them and apologized for having ignored his letters from England.

She had signed her letter, "Your loving friend."

But Frank never saw the letter, which had been returned to Carolyn unopened. The stamped message on the envelope indicated that he had moved. No forwarding address. In response, Carolyn telegrammed her friend Jeanne Morestal to learn what had become of him. On the day before Harold Burke happened into the Proper Pagan, Carolyn received from Jeanne the following response:

Dear Carolyn,

Well, I've done a little detective work of my own. Nobody knows for sure what's up with Frank. But you know how it works around here. Somebody's heard from somebody else who's heard from somebody else who's heard from somebody else who supposedly

has received a letter from Frank that explains every-
thing. . . . It's funny, but somehow, miraculously, this
little game of "telephone" turns out to be pretty
accurate most of the time. Don't you find that to be
true? So here goes.

You needn't feel guilty anymore, my dear. The rumor
about the Quarter is that Frank has left the country
(or "gone to the country," I'm not sure which) for an
unspecified amount of time "to be with" or "because
of" a woman named Nancy. The subtleties of the
French language make a translation of this passed-
along information somewhat imprecise, but the gen-
eral message, I think, is clear.

So you can stop worrying, my friend. You haven't de-
stroyed him, though I'm sure he'll never replace you.
How could he? None of your friends here have, that's
for sure. OK? He's not so special, see? He's just a
man like every other. You've been through enough
these past few months. If you ask me, it's about time
you started having a little fun over there on your side
of the pond!!!

We all miss you around here.

Love,
Jeanne

Frank's new girl. This Nancy something-or-other.

"I'd be delighted to have dinner with you," Carolyn had
answered when, at the Proper Pagan, Harold Burke asked her to
dinner.

A few days later, Harold offered her a job she could not turn down. Editor of the *Riverside Review*. Poetry, fiction, essays. She thought she might convince Scott Fitzgerald to let her have one of his early, unpublished stories (though she could never hope to pay Scott his usual rate). Perhaps even Hemingway would contribute. And new writers too, hers to discover. Harold was wise to offer Carolyn the job, she thought. She would make his journal a success. The position was everything she had ever wanted.

Everything in a position, that is.

Not everything in her life.

Naturally, she made clear to Harold that her acceptance of the job precluded relations with him of anything but a professional nature. But when he offered to accompany her to Boston to help her get settled in a new apartment she could hardly turn him down. It was, after all, his magazine. Still, she did not like the idea of boarding a train alone with Harold Burke. She feared it would make her sad. She feared it would make her think of Frank.

"Oh, I'll be there," Bess had promised. "To hold your hand and see you off."

But where was Bess now? Carolyn wondered.

Four o'clock.

Perhaps Bess had gone straight to the train station. Or perhaps she had met a doe-eyed Adonis from out of town and had altered her priorities.

Carolyn glanced at her suitcase. Packed.

Waiting.

Then a knock on the door.

She jumped at the sound. "Damn!" she whispered.

It could not be Bess, for she had a key. Harold.

"Just a minute," Carolyn called, standing and taking a deep breath. She moved to the center of the room, glancing about her, as if the details of the apartment might hold a clue as to what she should do next.

But there was only one thing to do.

She answered the door.

It was not Harold.

"Special delivery for Carolyn Keene," said the postman. "Are you Carolyn Keene?"

"Yes."

He handed her a box about the size of the New York City phone directory.

"Thank you," she said.

The box was wrapped in brown paper.

"Sign here, please," he said.

She signed, then closed the door.

The box had come from Paris.

Frank's handwriting.

She moved to the bedroom, closing the door behind her as if she were not already alone in the apartment.

She sat on the bed and tore at the paper.

When she first saw the typed manuscript of her abandoned mystery novel, she thought Frank cruel. Sure, she had left a few things behind at his apartment. Some clothes, books, magazines, even a spare pair of reading glasses. Nothing essential. He had not returned any of them. She had not asked for them. But now this? Her unfinished manuscript? It was the emblem of her failure, she believed, for which even her new position at the *Riverside Review* was mere consolation. What did Frank mean to communicate by this? She had never believed him capable of cruelty.

Perhaps his new lover had insisted he return it.

But then why didn't he just destroy it?

She wished she had left the apartment a few minutes earlier. Before the postman arrived. Then she noticed that the manuscript felt heavier than she remembered its having been before.

She flipped through the pages. The manuscript was longer. Different. She glanced at the last page. At the bottom was written: "THE END."

Finished.

But how?

After the last page was a handwritten note:

Dear Carolyn,

I don't know if this book is good or bad, but I remembered the things you told me about your heroine, Nancy, the girl-detective, and I've taken a few weeks away from the Quarter and everything else in my life to finish her story. The writing is my own. And yours. Of course, it doesn't make me the author of those Hemingway stories. Nothing can make those stories mine. But here's some writing for you. The best I can do. Something real anyway.

Damn, I know the second half of this book is not as good as the first, but at least it exists, and now it's yours to fix up any way you please.

Yours, any way you please,
Frank

By the time Carolyn heard another knock on the door she had read twenty pages of the new, second half of the book.

It was good.

Better than that.

She listened to more knocking, then more, then silence

followed by the sound of receding footsteps in the hall outside the apartment, rapping down the stairs, leading Harold
Burke away forever. She turned back to the mystery novel,
reading on, not stopping even to turn on a light after the sun
had set outside the bedroom window. She never missed its
light; the risen full moon, which shone through the glass,
proved illumination enough to get Carolyn all the way to the
end.

Hemingway held aloft his glass of champagne.

"To Frank and Carolyn!"

The other revelers at Le Dôme, who had gathered to celebrate
the Dixons' marriage—which took place less than an hour
before beneath a Delacroix mural in a chapel of St-Sulpice—
raised their glasses and turned toward the couple, who sat at
a long table upon which had been placed a vase of roses.

"To Frank and Carolyn!"

It had been three weeks since the completed manuscript
had arrived for Carolyn in Greenwich Village. Almost
immediately thereafter, she had booked passage on the S.S.
France. She had often been foolish in her life, she reflected.
But she was not always a fool. She loved Frank. She had the
means to go to him. Now she had the will.

Six days later, when Frank had met Carolyn at Le Havre,
the two had held to each other for a long time on the dock.
They had not let go of one another's hand on the train ride
into Paris nor even as they had climbed the staircase that led
to his new apartment on the Rue de l'Odéon. There, late-
afternoon light had streamed through the open window;
Frank and Carolyn had looked for a long time at one another,
not only to absorb the features of the other's face but to grasp
the almost-too-good-to-be-true notion that all of this was
real—the sound of the traffic outside, the overstuffed

comforter on the antique bed, the luggage in one corner, the being-together in the here and now.

"Say my name," Frank said.

"Frank," she answered.

"Carolyn," he said in turn.

Now they were wed.

"To the Dixons' sacred union!" Scott Fitzgerald proposed after rising to his feet at the end of the table opposite Hemingway. "That is," he continued, "if I can use the word 'union' without being accused of being political."

"Oh, no one ever accused you of that, Scott!" Dos Passos called from across the room.

"To their union," the room replied, drinking again.

This too was real, Frank and Carolyn reminded one another.

Next, Zelda Fitzgerald stood up beside her husband: "Enough about unions," she announced, hoisting a martini. "Let's drink to onions!" She had been tippling even more than Scott. "Elegant pearl onions!"

The revelers drank to her toast. "To onions!"

After the toasts, when scattered conversations once more arose throughout the café, Frank crossed the room to Hemingway, whose hand he shook in thanks for his generous toast.

"It's nothing more than the two of you deserve," Hemingway said.

"Well, Carolyn deserves the best, that's for sure," Frank said. "But as for me . . ." He stopped.

"You deserve the best too, old man."

Frank shrugged.

"Look, let's have no false modesty, understand, Frank? What I've always admired about you is that you maintain the lowest bullshit quotient of anybody living in the Quarter."

"I have a bit of a surprise for you in that regard."

"As regards bullshit?"

Frank nodded and led Hemingway to a quiet corner of the café where he confessed his part in the story of the lost suitcase (omitting the role of the theft's mastermind, Gertrude Stein, who sat now with Alice Toklas across the room).

Hemingway listened to the tale, his eyes narrowing.

"So, now you know the truth," Frank concluded. "I'm sorry to have kept it from you so long."

Hemingway nodded. He said nothing.

"So, uh, do we need to box now or something?" Frank asked.

"That damn suitcase."

"Yeah, damn."

"Did you read any of the stories inside?"

Frank nodded.

"What did you think?"

"I thought they were very good, but . . ."

"But what?"

"Somewhat inaccroachable."

Hemingway laughed. "I see Gertrude's gotten to you. Like she's gotten to everybody else."

Frank shrugged.

Hemingway put his heavy arms around Frank, pulling him close in a bear hug. "Here's what I want you to do, Frank," he whispered.

"Okay."

"Never breathe a word about this to anyone. Speculation about that damn suitcase has become widespread, which is never a bad thing in my business. Understand?"

"Sure."

"The writing was all horseshit anyway."

"Oh, now, I wouldn't go that far. . . ."

Hemingway stepped back, slapping Frank on the shoulder. He glanced across the room to Carolyn. "You got a good girl there, old boy."

"Damn right."

"And Frank, one more thing . . ."

"Yeah?"

"Were you kidding about the boxing?"

Frank nodded.

Hemingway shrugged and turned away.

Meanwhile, Carolyn sat with Gertrude and Alice. The two older women had spent most of the afternoon receiving their numerous acolytes.

"A fine turnout today," Gertrude said.

"You should have heard all the complimentary sentiments directed to Gertrude," Alice added without looking up from her needlepoint. "I declare, sometimes genius actually gets its due. Almost."

"And I think many of these folks were delighted to see you and Frank here as well," Gertrude added.

"Oh, well . . . that's kind of you to say."

"Did you come for a word of wisdom?" Gertrude asked.

"I came to say thank you for being here. And for everything."

"Well, you're welcome," Gertrude said.

"But I'll take your word of wisdom."

Gertrude considered. "Ah, I have so many words. Singly, in pairs, in all sorts of combinations."

"Indeed she does," Alice said. "You have no idea."

"Oh, I can imagine," Carolyn said.

Alice stopped working on her needlepoint and looked across the table to Carolyn. "No, really. You can't imagine."

Gertrude shrugged in mock modesty.

"Well, one word will do for now," Carolyn said.

"Amiably," Gertrude answered. "Yes. That's the word for you and Frank and your new situation."

"Amiably," Carolyn repeated.

"From the Latin *amicus*. Friend."

"Oh, that's quite nice. Like 'amiable'?"

"No, no!" Gertrude answered, slapping her hand on the table to underline her dissent. "'Amiably' is not like 'amiable,' my dear girl. 'Amiable' is boring. I would never give you an adjective. I think too highly of both you and Frank to do such a thing. Good Lord, an adjective like 'amiable' is suitable only to cud-chewing cows and opium eaters. No, I gave you an adverb, my dear girl, a word that describes action. It's not the same thing. One can't just be amiable. Who would want to be described in such a way? However, people in love must act amiably. Understand?"

"I believe I do."

Tourists who happened into the café left with wonder that Paris could be so lively on an ordinary day.

But this was no ordinary day.

Nor was it an ordinary night.

Around two a.m., Frank and Carolyn returned to their apartment. There, Carolyn gave to her new husband as a wedding gift a box of her own newly typed pages, a novel, companion piece to the girl-detective story that Frank had completed for her weeks before. She had written the book on a portable typewriter in her cabin aboard the S.S. *France*. The outline of the story had come easily; she recalled a yarn Frank once told her about a chest of valuables he and Joe had discovered in a railroad water tower not far from their home in Bayport. Carolyn had merely added a few villains and plot twists. The words themselves, however, were as hard won as ever. Carolyn suffered over each sentence. How could she not? Hadn't Hemingway told her that sentences needed to be the moon and stars? She did not believe she could ever create such weighty heavenly bodies from mere words; still, she hoped to make her sentences at least as ordered and self-possessed as summer clouds. As a result, she did not take more than one or two strolls about the deck of the S.S. *France* the whole voyage. Instead, she typed. And retyped. She slept very little. More typing, typing. By the time she finished her draft of the book, the ship was within sight of France. She was tired, but she thought she had never spent more fruitful hours.

"'Tower Treasure,'" Frank read aloud in their hotel room as he riffled the pages in the box.

She nodded. "It's a mystery box."

"A what?"

She touched the box that held the typed pages. "See? A box with a mystery in it."

"Ah, mystery box."

"Like the one you gave to me."

Frank kissed her, then set the title page face down on the bed and began reading the first page.

"Boy detectives," Carolyn volunteered. "Brothers."

"Joe and Frank," he read aloud. He stopped. His face grew serious. "Joe and me . . ." He turned back to her. "Do you know what you've given me?"

"Nothing more than you gave to me," she answered.

He could not speak.

"Besides, it's not just for you," she added.

"Oh?"

"It's for your nephew too. Joe's boy. Wherever he is. So

he can know something happy and adventurous about his father's past. And something about his Uncle Frank's past as well."

"But he doesn't know my name. He doesn't even know his father's real name."

"No matter," Carolyn said. "When he picks up the book in a shop or a library he'll know, deep inside. Even if the names and places in the book all seem to be made up. He'll know."

"And if he doesn't read this particular book?" Frank asked.

"We'll write others," she answered. "Lots. And books for girls too. One girl in particular."

"Your sister Rose?"

She nodded. "A life's work together, you and me, if you're interested."

Frank's answer was evident in his eyes.

Epilogue

For more than thirty years Frank and Carolyn coauthored their two series of mystery novels, which sold millions of copies and entertained generations of young readers all over the world. In 1959, their publisher chose to revise the two series, replacing words like "electric torch" with "flash-light," "gramophone" with "hi-fi record player," and "roadster" with "convertible," etc. Ghostwriters were engaged for the rewriting assignment; meanwhile, Frank and Carolyn embarked on a series of world travels, which they chronicled in three books of nonfiction that are now considered classics of the genre. In this manner they passed the remainder of their days happily together.

The Real Characters

Among the characters in *Mystery Box* are a number of historical literary figures. Their interactions with the fictional Frank Dixon and Carolyn Keene are, of course, wholly imagined; at the time of the novel's setting, however, these literary figures did live and work in Paris and were well acquainted with one another.

During this period, Ernest Hemingway wrote and published his first short stories and his first novel, *The Sun Also Rises*. Soon after his marriage to Hadley Richardson ended in 1926, he married Pauline Pfeiffer, a magazine editor. Hemingway left France in 1928 and in the following three decades traveled the world and lived with drama and fury. He was awarded the Nobel Prize for Literature in 1954.

While in France in 1924, F. Scott Fitzgerald wrote *The Great Gatsby*, his masterpiece. He and Zelda regularly visited the Villa America, the Mediterranean residence of Gerald and Sara Murphy, who later served as inspiration for the main characters in Fitzgerald's last completed novel, *Tender Is the Night*. The Fitzgeralds returned permanently to the United States in 1931, by then wearied and weakened by alcohol and mental illness. Zelda's last years were spent in a mental institution. Scott died in 1940 in Hollywood, California.

Gertrude Stein lived at 27 Rue de Fleurus with her partner, Alice Toklas, where the two women hosted many of the world's leading writers, artists, and musicians. There, Stein developed her experimental style of writing, exemplified by her books *The Making of Americans* and *Tender Buttons*. With the 1934 publication of *The Autobiography of Alice B. Toklas*, Stein's work gained wide public attention. She and Alice lived together in Paris until Gertrude's death in 1946. (Note: the Gertrude Stein quotation that serves as epigraph to *Mystery Box* is a literary invention.)

DATE DUE

FOLLETT